A PERFECT DAY
TO BE ALONE

T0349813

A PERFECT DAY
TO BE ALONE

Nanae Aoyama

Translated from the Japanese by
Jesse Kirkwood

MACLEHOSE PRESS
QUERCUS · LONDON

First published in Japan as ひとり日和 (*Hitori biyori*) by
Kawade Shobo Shinsha Ltd, Toyko, in 2007

First published in Great Britain in 2024 by

MacLehose Press
An imprint of Quercus
Carmelite House
50 Victoria Embankment
London EC4Y 0DZ

An Hachette UK company

A CIP catalogue record for this book is available from the British Library.

ISBN (MMP) 978 1 52942 768 4
ISBN (Ebook) 978 1 52942 769 1

7 9 10 8

Designed and typeset in Warnock by Patty Rennie
Printed and bound in Great Britain by Clays Ltd, Elcograf S.p.A.

MIX
Paper | Supporting
responsible forestry
FSC® C104740

Papers used by Quercus Books are from
well-managed forests and other responsible sources.

A PERFECT DAY
TO BE ALONE

SPRING

≕◆≕

It was raining when I arrived at the house.

The walls of my room were lined with cat photos, set in fancy frames just below the ceiling. They started on the left as you went in, continued above the window on the far side of the room and extended halfway down the right-hand wall. I didn't feel like counting them. Some were black and white and others colour. Some looked off to one side, while others seemed to stare me right in the eye. The whole room had the austere atmosphere of a family altar. I just stood there in the doorway.

"This is nice." I felt a tug on my crochet scarf and turned around to find the little old lady leaning in and squinting to inspect the stitching.

I pulled the cord for the ceiling light. *Ker-chick*. Fluorescent light filled the room. Standing by her at the window she'd opened, I looked out over the hedge of the small garden. On the other side of the narrow street I could see the station platform. A mild breeze was blowing, and a fine drizzle caressed my face.

For a moment, we just stood there in silence. Then there was a chime, followed by a platform announcement.

"Train's coming," she said. The deep, pale wrinkles that lined her face seemed suddenly more pronounced, and I backed away from her slightly.

"Well, this is your room," she said, and walked off, just like that.

I remember thinking: She looks like she's barely got a week to live.

I hadn't bothered introducing myself properly when I arrived. It had just seemed too embarrassing. I wasn't in the habit of going around declaring my name to people like that. Nor was I used to others actually calling me by it.

From the small station, I had followed the map my mum had drawn for me, making my way to the house as slowly as I could. My hair was damp from the drizzle and stuck to my cheeks. Even in my woollen winter cardigan, scarf wrapped tightly around my neck, I felt a chill. It was the middle of April, but there still hadn't been a single warm day all year. I set my duffle bag down on the side of the road and tried to find my folding umbrella, but it had disappeared among the densely packed layers of clothes and cosmetics. As I rummaged around in the bag, the tissues I had squeezed in at the last minute went scattering across the pavement.

My mum's map looked like she'd copied it straight from a street atlas: even the smallest alleyways were there in painstaking detail. Below, in her old-fashioned rounded handwriting, she'd left me a series of unnecessarily detailed instructions – things like *Leave the station by the north exit and go straight down the shopping arcade*, or *Turn left at the corner with the orthopaedic clinic*. I wrinkled my nose. Clearly she still worried about me, whatever she might say. It didn't matter that I'd turned twenty: to her, I was still a naïve young woman, the kind who'd get all anxious and emotional as soon as she was left to fend for herself. When I imagined her sitting in the dimly lit living room after I'd gone to bed, writing out these directions and thinking to herself ah, yes, now *this* is motherly love, I couldn't help smirking.

The damp air had turned the cheap copy paper soggy. I rubbed it with the side of my thumb, so that the writing smudged. Then I rubbed it some more, using my whole hand this time, until all that was left was a grey smear.

I'd said goodbye to my mum that morning at Shinjuku station. "Take care then," she'd said, patting my head and shoulders. I just muttered "Mm-hm" over and over, scratching my bottom, with no idea where to look. We were standing right in front of the ticket gates, and commuters kept jostling us and glaring as they passed. I tried to take her by the arm and move us out of the way, but she seemed to have stiffened up. I pretended not to notice and glanced at the departure board above the ticket gates. Then, before she could say whatever it was she was about to say, I blurted out, "Well, good luck with everything!" and, with a quick wave, hurried off through the ticket gate, down the stairs, and onto the train. Even after the train picked up speed, I could feel her eyes boring into me from behind.

Walking from the station to the house, I passed three middle-aged women coming the other way. With their fluttering white blouses and shoulder-padded jackets, they looked like they were off to shop at a department store or something. They were walking side by side, even though that meant they couldn't all fit on the pavement. As I passed them, I caught a strong whiff of perfume. It was not unpleasant: artificial, cloying, and yet somehow nostalgic. I felt suddenly lonely, in the anxious way that nostalgia always seemed to trigger. The shoes they were all wearing, more like indoor slippers really, looked incredibly comfortable. Glancing at a nearby shoe shop, I saw several similar pairs lined up in the window.

I turned at the orthopaedic clinic, walked down several narrow alleys, and at the end of the last one found the house. The gate's paint was peeling, and from it hung a red basket that seemed to serve as a letterbox. Though the house stood directly opposite one end of the station platform, you had to take the long way round and walk down the shopping arcade to reach it. There was also a path that ran parallel to the platform, but the garden hedge prevented access to the house from that side.

There was no sign outside to indicate who lived there. On the other side of the gate, a path led to the back garden, though half of it was taken up by plant pots of various sizes that seemed to be filled with nothing but soil. Like the gate, the walls of the house were peeling, creating a mottle of red and black. On one side of the front door was a recessed grey washbasin and a stack of buckets. On the other stood a camellia tree so tall its branches brushed against the roof of the single-storey house. It was oddly magnificent, its dark green leaves glistening in the rain, dotted with large pink flowers. I hadn't realised they bloomed at this time of year.

I don't want to go in. I tried saying the words out loud, like I really meant them, but as soon as they left my mouth they sounded false. The fact was, I didn't really care. It wasn't even a question of wanting or not wanting to go in. I'd been told to come, so here I was. And, if it meant I could live in Tokyo, anywhere would do.

After showing me to my room, the old lady brought me some tea and then set about various tasks: helping me unpack the cardboard boxes I'd had delivered earlier, starting the washing machine, making dinner, running the bath. While we were unpacking the boxes, we made small talk about the weather and how safe the area was. I didn't exactly try to get the conversation flowing.

Watching her from behind as she extracted my clothes from the boxes, unfolding and then refolding them, I told myself, with a wince, that she was probably going to require some looking after.

Just as the conversation had fizzled out and an awkward silence was looming, she left the room. I breathed in deep, right into the pit of my stomach, then out again. I stayed in the room until she called to say it was time to eat.

Dinner turned out to be pretty plain and insubstantial.

"Want some more?"

"Oh – please."

I gave her my bowl. It came back piled high with rice.

"Glad to see you can eat."

"Um, yeah . . ." I replied, taking the bowl and tucking in. A few more side dishes wouldn't have gone amiss, I thought.

"I eat plenty myself too, mind!" she exclaimed, heaping rice into her own bowl. I made another interested noise while I crunched on a pickle.

"Shall I put the television on?"

I found myself staring at the wrinkles on her hand as she scrabbled for the remote control.

"Not that there's much on . . ."

She flicked through the channels for a while before eventually settling on a baseball game. Then she carried on eating without giving the television a second glance.

At her age, I thought, listening was probably more fun than watching.

Instead of chomping away noisily at her food, she ate quietly. I didn't know much about how old people lived, but I'd come here determined not to be fazed by any generation gap between us. And yet she was turning out to be surprisingly normal. For dessert, she brought out some home-made coffee flavour jellies, drizzling a spiral of creamer onto them in what was clearly a well-practised motion.

After dinner, I stayed under the kotatsu blanket, though its built-in heater wasn't on. I gazed mindlessly at the television for a while, then tried to read the book I'd brought with me. What exactly were you supposed to talk about on your first night at someone's house? I found myself re-reading the same line over and over.

It still didn't feel like I was actually going to live with her. Even though I'd shown up here of my own accord, I felt intensely uncomfortable, like a kid who's been left at a neighbour's house until dinner.

On the television, the commentator was blabbering away excitedly.

"You a baseball fan, Chizu?"

Hearing my own name gave me a jolt. It had been a while since someone actually called me by it, and it put me on edge, like some kind of bad omen.

"Actually I . . . don't know much about it."

"Oh! *Now* you tell me."

I laughed awkwardly in response.

"I thought it might be something you'd enjoy," she said before abruptly turning off the television. Then she reached into the pocket of her smock for her knitting needles and wool and began working away at a small ball-like object.

On the table was a dessert plate piled with salami sticks. I was already full, but the silence was unbearable and I didn't know what else to do with myself, so I nibbled on one. Its salty flavour filled my mouth. When one of her cats showed up and started mewing, she spat the stick she was chewing on into her hand and fed it to the animal.

"Hope you won't mind living with an old crone like me. My name's Ginko Ogino, by the way."

So now we were doing introductions. I jumped at the chance to revive the conversation.

"Chizu Mita. Thank you for letting me stay."

"So, do you mind if I go ahead and jump in?"

"Sorry?"

"The bath. I like to go first."

"Oh. Sure, go ahead."

"Then I'll hop right in."

Once she'd left the room, I lay down on the floor where I'd been sitting. At least she doesn't seem too uptight, I thought, beginning to relax slightly. It was going to make things a lot easier if, instead of fussing over me, she just treated me like a daughter who had overstayed her welcome in the parental nest. Cringing as I noticed the vague smile still plastered across my face, I tugged my cheeks back into a more normal position. The ginger cat that had eaten the salami stick was eyeing me warily from the corner of the room.

As soon as I heard the sound of water slopping around in the bathroom, I set about rooting through all the drawers I could find, starting in the kitchen. None of them were particularly full; instead, each seemed to house its own modest collection of objects. The one under the sink was empty except for two pairs of cooking chopsticks. In the underfloor storage space I found three large bottles of what looked like home-distilled plum wine. The date *21 June '95* had been scrawled with a marker on each of their red plastic caps.

While I was at it, I decided to have a look in her room, across the corridor from my own. Alongside the brown, chequered curtains dangled a string of faded paper cranes. Looking closer, I realised they were all made from what looked like old pamphlets of some kind. I gave them a quick shake, producing a swirl of dust. There was also a small Buddhist altar, but I tried not to look at that too closely.

On top of a small chest of drawers was a glass cabinet. Inside, behind tight ranks of miniature old-fashioned cars, a Tokyo Tower replica and a model of some castle or other, there was a set of those Russian dolls. The ones where each doll contains another doll inside it – what were they called again? I recognised them because my uncle had once brought some back from a business trip to what was then still the Soviet Union.

So, this is how old people live, I thought. As I was looking around the room with my arms folded, I heard the bathroom door creak open. I opened the glass cabinet, grabbed the wooden clown doll that happened to be closest to hand, and retreated to my own room. I went and stood by the window and started jiggling the doll around at my side, waiting for a train to pull in at the station. Almost immediately, its head fell off.

I lay down on the pale green tatami and, almost nuzzling the mat with my nose, gave it a deep sniff. Next to me, a futon had been laid out with what looked like fresh bedding.

I rolled onto my back and stared up at the cat photos lining the walls, considering each in turn. I had fun giving them names: *Buchi* for the tabby. *Madara* for the spotty one. *Kuro*, which just meant "black". *Mi-ke* for the tortoiseshell. *Chamimi* ("brown ears"), *Akahana* ("red nose"), *Kobutori* ("pudgy"). And so on. I counted them. Twenty-three photos. What was with these cats? It was a question I'd somehow been unable to ask during dinner, or when Ginko was showing me the room.

I closed my eyes and thought of all the days to come.

"So I've moved in with this old lady."

"Oh yeah?" Yohei replied, his eyes still glued to the

screen. He was playing mah-jong on the computer. Words like *pong* and *chow* would pop up on the screen, their meanings completely lost on me, and he would grunt things like "Crap!" or "No way!" in response. He seemed pretty into it.

We hadn't seen each other at all in the two weeks since I'd moved in with Ginko, but judging from the look on his face when I arrived, he'd have preferred it to be even longer. His place was an hour and a half, and three changes of train, from Ginko's – a journey so tedious it had put me off coming until today. Now all I wanted was for him to at least acknowledge my good deed in making the trek.

"Why can't I just move in here?"

I tried pinching his back, ruffling up his hair, even licking his ear, but he didn't reply. "You can't stand me, can you?"

"What?" Yohei couldn't have sounded more irritated. He still wasn't looking at me.

"Never mind. I'm off. Can't keep the old lady waiting, can I!"

Even after I snatched my bag and stormed out, slamming the door behind me, there was no response from Yohei. I waited outside for a moment, mobile phone in hand, but eventually, hounded by the chilly spring wind and my own sense of failure, I ran back to the station.

White petals were fluttering down onto me from the cherry trees in front of the station. It was depressing. What was the point in a season like spring that couldn't make its mind up? Even when it was sunny, there was always that lingering chill in the air, like the weather was making fun of you. Everything would be so much easier if winter just segued straight into summer. When I heard people talking about all their picnics under the cherry blossoms, or how delicious the fuki buds or the nano-hana shoots or the freshly harvested onions were, I felt like yelling at them to take it down a notch. I'd find myself going out of my way to show that I, for one, wasn't so easily taken in. Anyway, I was irritable enough already: the medicine I took for my pollen allergy made my throat relentlessly dry, no matter how many times I swallowed, and when I sniffed my snot, it tasted weirdly of blood.

Yohei and I had been seeing each other for two and a half years, but we never went out on dates. The previous year we hadn't even exchanged birthday presents. We'd usually just hang out at his apartment, and while our conversation wasn't exactly thrilling, we didn't get into any spectacular arguments either. It was a bit like when people say their partner is the air they breathe, except that in our case, we would have done just fine without each other, so I suppose the metaphor didn't really hold up. I didn't know why or how we'd break up, but it did feel like the end was coming. And if it was going to happen anyway, I was happy to let things take their natural course. There didn't seem much point in trying to speed things up.

He'd been in the year above me at school and was

now studying something called systems engineering at university. He wasn't very serious about it, and mainly just sat in his apartment playing video games. I would sit there watching him from behind, reading books, or just letting my thoughts drift. When he'd reached a certain point in his game he would stop and we'd have sex – fumbling, childish sex. About a third of the time, I'd turn him down.

When I got back to the house, Ginko was sitting under the kotatsu blanket, doing some embroidery. The blanket's unusual thickness was explained by the fact that it was actually a series of different blankets: a heavily pilled beige one followed by a brown one, and on top of that a red feather quilt.

"I'm back."

"Oh, hello again," replied Ginko, pushing the reading glasses that had slipped down her nose into place. Trying to block out the memory of my pathetic exchange with Yohei, I flashed her a good-natured smile as I slipped my jacket onto a hanger.

"Fancy some yokan?"

"Oh, yes please."

Ginko gave a little grunt of acknowledgement and got to her feet. After setting the kettle on the stove, she stood rooted to the spot, her left hand on the back of a chair, her right hand on her hip. I went and stood next to her and gazed vacantly through the small window above the sink at the narrow street outside. Faced with this unchanging scene, I found myself letting my guard down slightly, and muttered:

"Things haven't been great recently."

"Oh?"

I couldn't be bothered going into any more detail, and just gave a vague chuckle instead. Ginko responded with one of her own.

On the corner of the kitchen table was a long, half-eaten stick of yokan bean cake, poking out from its cellophane wrapping.

"Shall I cut us some?" I offered.

"*Water boiling in an empty kitchen – is there anything so sad?*"

"Sorry?"

"Don't you think that's nice?"

"What . . . is it?"

"A haiku. My niece won third prize for it in middle school."

"*Water boiling* . . . wait, how did it go?"

"*Water boiling in an empty kitchen – is there anything so sad?*"

"Right. Sort of . . . melancholy, isn't it?"

I took a fruit knife and began cutting the yokan into thin, even slices, like I was cutting up a crab stick. All of a sudden, I felt in better spirits. If only everything could be resolved with this little fuss, I thought. With such clean, decisive strokes.

Ginko was still standing there with her hand on her hip. She was short and thin, with soft, curly white hair that ran down to her shoulders like it had simply been left to grow. She always wore an ochre-coloured smock, and held herself erect, her back straight. Something about her reminded me of a neatly compressed rice ball. In her front pockets she carried her knitting needles, a ball of wool the colour of dishwater and, from time to time, the ginger cat, which was really still a kitten. It was named Cha-iro, or "Ginger"; the other one, with black stripes, had the equally inventive name of Kurojima, or "Black Stripes". The two were completely unrelated.

When we'd finished our tea, Ginko returned to her embroidery. Apparently afternoons were for embroidery and evenings for knitting. I peered closer to see what she was working on.

"Is that a slipper?"

"That's right. Weren't you saying you liked this Miffy character?"

Now that she mentioned it, I did vaguely remember the topic coming up at dinner the other night. Apparently, she'd gone straight out to a nearby clothes shop and bought a pair of Miffy slippers, and was now painstakingly stitching another rabbit right next to the original one.

"Two for the price of one."

"Sorry?"

"You get two Miffies for the price of one," she said.

"Oh. Right . . ."

She showed me the slipper. Her Miffy was skinnier than the original, with a narrower mouth and eyes. It had a sort of mournful expression.

I decided it was time to ask the question that had been weighing on my mind.

"Those cats – were they all yours at one point?"

"Cats? Which cats?"

"The ones in my room. You know, all the photos."

"Ah, those. Well, that's the Cherokee room."

"It's the . . . what?"

"The photos on the walls. I call them the Cherokees."

"Cherokees? . . . Is that, like, a special name for dead cats?"

"No, it's just that, well . . ." She paused. "I forget their real names."

"Oh. Huh."

"Sad, isn't it. See, Cherokee was my first cat. My niece brought him in off the street. And now he's the only one whose name I can remember."

I laughed at this, but inside I felt uneasy, as if I'd stumbled across some dark truth.

I'd assumed old people were always early risers, but I soon learned that wasn't the case. Some days Ginko would get up after me. On those mornings, instead of making something like tamagoyaki or miso soup that would require actual cooking, I would just grab one of the bread rolls that were lying around and have it with a cup of tea or something. I never made anything for Ginko. On the other hand, if she happened to get up earlier, she would always leave something out for me, and I'd heat it up. Instead of wrapping whatever she'd made with cling film, she would just cover it with a plate or something. Everything she made tasted blander than my mum's version of the same dish. She made her own miso soup stock by just boiling a load of dried sardines.

It was only that first night that she rushed around playing the host. Now she pretty much let me fend for myself. She would leave dishes unwashed for days at a time, and she clearly wasn't very enthusiastic about hoovering, because there were cat hairs all over the place. I tried just ignoring all this for a while, but one day, unable to help myself, I gave the whole house a clean. Ginko didn't say thank you or anything, which left me feeling a little put out, but I decided not to bring it up. She seemed so blithely unconcerned by the whole thing that it was hard to really care myself.

She didn't seem very passionate about the garden either. The dandelions and daisies were very cute and all, but other, more mysterious weeds had sprouted in the corners and were steadily gaining ground. It looked like things might get out of hand in the summer. At the same time, I found myself imagining the same scene in winter, a sprawl of faded brown weeds that nobody had bothered to deal with. At the end of the garden was a sweet olive tree, to which Ginko had fastened one end of a laundry pole.

From the station came the constant sound of trains and platform announcements. When an express service hurtled past without stopping, the house's windows would rattle and clatter, but I soon got used to it. If anything, it was probably healthy for a barely employed youngster like me and an old lady like Ginko to have that level of noise in the background. When I brushed my teeth in the morning, I would stand on the veranda, hand on my hip, and watch the trains go by. Sometimes I would make eye contact with a passenger, but when I carried on staring they were always quick to avert their gaze.

From Ginko's house you could only see the last carriage of the Shinjuku-bound trains. There was just one set of ticket gates, and they were at the other end of the station to the house, so hardly anyone ventured this far along to wait for their train. The path that ran between the garden hedge and the platform came to a dead end in front of the house, and random strangers would occasionally come wandering along, glance around with a bewildered expression, and then turn back the way they had come.

Before coming here, I lived with my mum. Her and dad got divorced when I was five, and since then it had just been the two of us. There were times when I felt sorry for myself for having an absent father. At one point, I had

even flirted with the idea of becoming a proper delin-
quent, but I gave that up when I realised I wasn't very
good at it. I tried blaming my bad moods on my parents,
but that just led to tedious, drawn-out conversations,
and in the end my adolescence had simply fizzled out
with everything still up in the air.

As for my dad, who had moved to Fukuoka for work,
I hadn't seen him for almost two years. If he came to
see me in Tokyo then I'd probably say hello, but I wasn't
planning on going out of my way to visit him.

Mum taught Japanese at a private secondary school
and was going to China as part of a teacher exchange
programme. She had first mentioned the idea at the end
of the previous year. And she had graciously invited me,
her daughter who had done nothing but cycle through
part-time jobs since graduating from high school, to join
her.

"So, fancy it?" she had asked, biting into a slab of chocolate that she'd only half-loosened from its foil wrapper.

"I'm good, thanks."

"Oh, come on."

"No way, Mum."

"What are you going to do here on your own?"

"I'll move to Tokyo. And . . . get a job."

I felt immediately embarrassed by what I'd said, and
poured some hot water straight into my empty mug from
the kettle.

"Wrong way round," she remarked, pushing the jar of

instant coffee in my direction as she went on. "Anyway, Tokyo and Saitama are basically the same place."

"They're definitely not."

"Why don't you just commute to Tokyo from here?"

"Mum, that's like a two-hour round trip. Not happening."

"Why Tokyo all of a sudden, anyway?"

"I'm just *going*, okay."

"Chizu, you don't know what living in a big city is like. You'll just end up exhausted, and then you'll come running back here. Plus the rent and everything is so much more expensive there."

"You just said it was basically the same place. I'm going, okay? Even before you started talking about going to China, I was thinking of moving out this year anyway. So everyone's a winner. I'm a grown-up now, Mum, I don't need babysitting."

I said all this without stopping for breath, then stared right at her. After a pause, she said, "You really think life's one big picnic, don't you?"

I didn't know what to say to that. Apparently convinced she'd won the argument, she took another emphatic bite of the chocolate. I did my best to look indifferent and fiddled with my earlobe.

"Well, if you aren't coming with me, then I'm sorry, but you'll have to earn your own keep. That, or go to university. There's only so long I can keep supporting you."

"University?"

"Yes, that's the deal. If you'll at least do that, I can send you a bit of money."

"Guess I'll earn my own keep then," I shot back. I really didn't want to be a student.

She kept on grumbling about this and that, but I remained silent until, eventually, she relented.

"Well, if that's really what you want, then I guess I can't stop you." Then, finally, she mentioned that she knew someone with a house in Tokyo who I could probably arrange something with. She was looking at me like some second-rate estate agent pitching a deal. Was this motherly love, or just a veiled attempt to keep me under her thumb? She's so weird, I thought as I sipped my lukewarm coffee.

"I only met her a few times when I was young, but all our Kanazawa relatives know her well. Whenever someone's daughter decides to move to Tokyo, she's always the one to host them until they find their feet."

"Huh. So she's like a sort of Tokyo godmother?"

"Well, parents worry, don't they? Sending their kid off on their own like that. Not to mention how much it all costs. Anyway, she's nice. Shouldn't give you much trouble. Actually, she must be getting pretty old these days, now that I think about it."

"Does she live on her own?"

"Yes. I think her husband died when she was young."

"And you never stayed with her?"

"Well, I was supposed to, when I first moved to Tokyo.

But then when I actually went to meet her, I just couldn't stand the cat smell. I ended up crashing at your father's place instead."

"The . . . cat smell?"

"Shame really, as I'd actually been looking forward to living with her. Anyway, I bet she could do with some company. I might as well give her a ring."

"You sure it's okay, suddenly imposing on her like this?"

"It can't hurt to ask. Anyway, she's family. I always send her a New Year's card. Rice crackers too, last year. Remember all those squid-flavoured ones your uncle in Nagoya sent us? I sent some of those on to her."

Mum got up and started poking around for her address book. Thinking I'd check the television listings, I grabbed the newspaper from her side of the table, sending the crumbs from her chocolate scattering. I swept them in the direction of her chair.

The next day, as I was clocking off from my part-time job, I found a message on my phone from her.

She says you can stay, it said. *Alright then*, I texted back.

I'd heard you needed at least a hundred thousand yen to rent a place of your own in Tokyo, plus there'd be all the hassle of setting up the utilities. Everything would be easier this way. As for Mum, maybe she was trying to purge whatever guilt she still felt about never staying at the house by foisting that responsibility onto me instead.

The lady turned out to be in her seventies already. She was the wife of my maternal grandmother's brother. I had no idea what that made her in relation to me. Mum kept referring to her as obachan, or auntie, and it wasn't until later that I found out her name was Ginko.

"So, I hear you're off to university?"

The words startled me. Ginko was gripping her reading glasses with one hand as she scanned the contents of a letter. Through the paper I could make out my mum's firm, round handwriting.

She'd been away for a month already, but this was her first letter. Arriving back from the local ward office where I'd just registered as a new resident, I found it in the red basket at the gate, wedged between a Pizza Hut flier and a newsletter titled *Yasuko Sunaga's Ward Administration Bulletin*.

"That's what your mother says, anyway."

"Right . . ."

"So you're going to be a student?"

"Nope."

"But studying is . . ."

"No, Ginko, I'm not going to university."

A separate letter addressed to me was lying on a corner of the low table. It felt like our conversation was being sucked up by the television screen. It was showing a programme about a sushi place at the Tsukiji Market that did really fresh fish at low prices. By now we were

25

both paying more attention to the television than each other.

"Hey, that looks pretty tasty. Do you like sushi, Ginko?"

"Oh, yes. Been a while since I last had some, though."

"Why don't we try that place? We could go tomorrow."

"Tomorrow?"

"It said they open at seven in the morning."

"I don't know about getting up that early . . ."

"You mean you can't be bothered?"

"Oh, it's not that."

"I guess seven in the morning *is* a bit much, isn't it . . . ?"

With a rice cracker wedged in her mouth, Ginko insisted that wasn't the reason, but in any case she clearly wasn't keen. She seemed to have something else to add, so I looked at her expectantly, but before I knew it the conversation seemed to have come to an end.

The silence that kept descending whenever we were in the same room was really starting to get to me. When it went on for too long, I'd start feeling somehow responsible for it. After finishing our meal, we'd have a brief conversation, and then, once the silence became too unbearable, I'd either get up and wordlessly walk off, pretend to be focusing on the television, or lie down on my side like I was taking a nap.

"Well, guess I should head to work!" I announced, making a conscious effort to sound lively as I started gathering my things.

The day after I arrived at the house, I had registered for part-time work with a company that provided hostesses for banquets and parties. I was taking the job pretty seriously and decided to tell myself that was why visiting Yohei felt like such a hassle. It had been a fortnight or so since we'd last seen each other, but I didn't seem to be missing him much.

The job paid eight thousand yen for two hours' work. I'd go round dinner parties pouring drinks, dishing out plates of salad, and singing karaoke duets with older men. I was glad to be making that much money. This way, I reckoned I'd have a million yen saved up by the following spring. Much more than Yohei, it was the prospect of seeing that figure in my bank account that really brought a smile to my face.

Today's event started at seven in the evening. That meant I had to be at the company's office in Chofu by half five, where I'd get changed, do my make-up, attend a briefing, and then go and get the banquet hall ready. I hadn't told Ginko I worked as a hostess. I figured she wouldn't even understand the concept, so I'd just told her I was washing dishes at a banquet hall. If I'd really talked her through everything the job entailed, she'd probably conclude it was some sleazy operation. I didn't want to have to defend my choices, and in any case I was planning on moving out as soon as I had some cash saved up. In the meantime, I just wanted to enjoy myself and avoid rocking the boat too much.

✻

The cats weren't taking to me very well.

Kurojima was a black-striped mongrel, his glossy coat patterned like snake scales. He had yellow eyes, an impressively bushy tail, and emitted a pungent, feral sort of odour. Sometimes he would catch a mouse, bring it over, and then torment it in front of you. Ginko would say, "Oh, stop that!" and make a show of shooing him away. But the mouse, by now dead and no longer of interest to the cat, would be left lying there indefinitely, meaning that at some point before dinner I had to take it to a corner of the garden and bury it. That wasn't really something I wanted to do, and I'd do my best to pretend I hadn't noticed it lying there, but somehow the task always ended up falling to me. When I finally shot Ginko a look and said, "You know there's a dead mouse lying there, right?", for some reason it felt like she'd won. I wondered whose job this had been until I showed up. It wasn't like Kurojima was going to get rid of the mice on his own, so I suppose Ginko must have disposed of them somehow. I didn't mind doing the actual burial. But when I picked up the little body, caked here and there with brown blood, and wrapped it in tissue, I'd get a momentary flush of goosebumps along my arms. Maybe this was the kind of thing you became desensitised to as you grew older.

The other cat, Cha-iro, had a thick ginger coat and a small bell around her neck. She was still a kitten really, and Ginko had a habit of shoving her into the pocket of her smock whenever she felt like it. Judging from the faint mewling coming from inside the pocket, the cat didn't particularly enjoy this, but I couldn't be bothered pointing this out to Ginko and resigned myself to pitying the creature from a distance.

Would these cats eventually end up like the others, I wondered, their photos lost among the "Cherokees" lining the walls of my room?

I'd been living with her for barely a month, but I was starting to feel like Ginko might be a little cold-hearted. Yes, she'd given all those girls from Kanazawa a place to stay, but how many of them did she even remember? It was depressing to imagine that I might be forgotten soon, too. I'd find myself about to mutter something about how hard it was to know what old people were thinking, only to stop short when I realised that I also didn't care.

It didn't really bother me what a frail old lady like Ginko thought of me. By the time you got to her age, I told myself, you were probably only capable of vague, approximate emotions anyway.

At the end of what had been a warm and pleasant May, it suddenly began to rain. Just as I was thinking that spring really didn't know when to call it quits, Ginko fell ill. She spent the whole day lying on her futon.

"You okay?" I asked, kneeling by her side.

"I'm fine."

"Shouldn't you see a doctor?"

"No, I'll be alright."

"We can call one and they'll come and have a look at you, won't they?"

Ginko didn't reply.

"Have you taken any medicine?"

"No."

"Don't you have a prescription or something? Like, some pills you always have knocking around?"

"This negi onion around my neck and a good sleep, that's all I need. Nothing fancy. The negi will sort me right out."

Well, that explained the smell in the room. Peering closer at her, I saw that she had taken a thick stick of the long, spring onion-like vegetable, crushed it and wrapped it around her neck together with a towel.

Soon, Ginko stopped replying completely. Inside, I was starting to panic. What if she actually died on me? I had no idea what you were supposed to do with an old person when they got sick.

That evening I decided to look in on her once every hour or so. Peeking through the gap in the sliding door, I was just able to make out the sound of her steady breathing. The room still stank of negi, but now there was some other smell mixed in with it, one I'd never come across before. The smell of the unwell, I thought to myself.

At three in the morning, I got up, waited for my eyes to adjust to the dark, and went back into her room.

Kneeling quietly at her side, I waved a hand in front of her face to check she was asleep. I could feel her breath, faint and damp against my fingers.

I got up and walked over to the glass cabinet on top of the chest of drawers, leaning in close to inspect its contents. Maybe all this cheap-looking junk means something to the old lady, I thought. There was also a small, mirrored nightstand by Ginko's futon, and on my way out of the room I stopped to pull out one of its rattan drawers and thrust my hand inside. Between what felt like paper and the cool surface of something plastic, I came across a small box covered in some kind of cloth that was pleasant to the touch. I slipped it out of the drawer and into my pocket. Ginko was still breathing away steadily.

I went to the kitchen, switched on the light above the sink, and downed a glass of water. Some of it spilled out of my mouth and onto the collar of my pyjamas. Outside, it was still raining. I closed my eyes and listened to the rain. Then I found myself thinking of a horror film I'd seen on television the other day and gave a little involuntary shudder.

To distract myself from thoughts of ghosts, I held the box I'd just taken up to the light and studied it. It was made from green imitation velvet, with an embroidered white rose in the centre of the lid, and inside was a necklace set with small green gems. It looked a little tawdry under the fluorescent sink light. I tried putting it on, but that felt wrong somehow, and soon I returned it to the box. As I turned to head back to my room, I noticed that there were now two glasses in the sink. She was able to come and get water by herself, then. On a whim, I opened up the rice cooker and found the remains of the previous day's bamboo rice, which I wrapped in cling film and put in the fridge.

Back in my room, I retrieved a shoebox from the wardrobe and placed the necklace box inside, where it joined the clown doll I'd taken on the first night. The box was full of other bits of junk – pencils, duck-shaped paperclips and the like, all tumbling around aimlessly.

My habit of pinching things started when I was young.

I wasn't brave enough to steal anything from a shop, though. Instead, I'd found a childish pleasure in taking tiny things from those around me and adding them to my collection. I wasn't collecting fancy pencil cases or brand-new trainers, only objects devoid of any value or importance – a motley assortment of rubbers, pencils, paperclips and so on. To me it was like taking a commemorative photo. As I retrieved these little objects that had been dropped on the floor or abandoned on a desk and slipped them into the pockets of my uniform, I would tell myself that I wasn't stealing, I was *collecting*, and that would ease my guilt. The fact that no-one even seemed to notice only made it more fun, although it also infuriated me that people could be so careless with their possessions.

Even now, that old habit still reared its head from time to time.

I used empty shoeboxes to hoard all the junk I had collected. There were three of them at the back of the wardrobe right now.

Whenever the fancy took me, I'd get the boxes out and immerse myself in nostalgia. Recalling each item's owner, I'd feel a wave of sadness, or chuckle softly to myself. The presence of the objects in my hand was always strangely comforting.

Then, after this stroll through my memories, I'd start hurling insults at myself in an eruption of self-loathing: *Thief! Coward! Freak!* When I did so, I could almost feel my skin thickening in real time.

I wanted to become immune to even the harshest insults. This was all just training, I would tell myself as I put the lids back on the shoeboxes.

Ginko stayed in bed for three days. But by the morning of the fourth, she was back to her usual self.

To be honest, I was pretty relieved. It had got to the point where I was thinking I might have to arrange her funeral – big bouquets, that kind of thing – just because I happened to be her lodger.

Sunday was a sunny, twenty-eight-degree day. The misery of spring was finally behind us, and I could go out in short sleeves. I was in such high spirits that I decided to pay Yohei an overdue visit on the way to my hostess job. When I opened the door using the spare key he'd given me, I was greeted by the sight of a girl I'd never seen before sitting at his feet in her underwear.

"Oh."

I was too surprised to say anything else.

"Oh." Yohei, in his grubby tank top, imitated me idiotically as he watched this unexpected encounter unfold. Even at a time like this, I couldn't help admiring his tanned arms.

The girl was all made up, her hair gathered up in a stylish top knot. As for me, I'd been planning on getting changed and doing my make-up once I got to work, so there I was in some random old T-shirt, my hair shoved back in a bun, and not a dab of make-up on my face.

This is it, I thought to myself. The reason for our break-up.

The girl was looking sheepishly down at the floor.

"Unbelievable," I said.

Yohei was smiling weirdly at me.

"You make me sick."

With that, I walked back out of his apartment. Our relationship seemed to have ended even more abruptly than I'd expected. I supposed this was things taking their natural course, just like I'd wanted. I'd told Yohei he made me sick, but on reflection, I wasn't sure my feelings even merited a line like that. I wasn't heartbroken, and nor was I particularly angry. If anything, it felt like I was heading home from an end-of-term exam.

On my way to the station, I stopped and looked around. The street seemed to be filled with couples and families. Ahead of me, a couple in school uniforms were linking arms, their bodies squeezed up against each other like they were trying to form an airtight seal. I sat on the edge of a raised flower bed and tried giving them all nasty looks, but nobody returned my gaze.

What did people actually mean when they said they were in love? Whatever it was that was bringing all these people together and keeping them there, it was a complete mystery to me. In any case, I had the feeling that the couples filing past me were experiencing something different from whatever I'd been doing all this time. How was I supposed to prevent the excitement of every new relationship from curdling into boredom? Was it even possible to stay together without that happening?

Unlike the last time I'd been here, there wasn't a single cherry blossom petal to be seen. Instead, when I looked up through the fresh summer leaves, I could see patches of sky so bright that I couldn't tell if they were blue or white. Everything was so dazzling it felt like it might give me a rash. Instead of sunshine and breezes, I wanted to feel the harsh wind of winter, the kind that mercilessly strips the moisture from your skin.

The people trooping down the street without even a glance in my direction looked like figures in a pencil sketch – scraps of paper that might, at any moment, be scattered by the warm breeze. But before I knew it, I could feel those flimsy scraps making shallow cuts in my skin. I sighed, folded my arms tightly across my chest, and, eyes downcast, set off at a brisk pace.

That evening I was working at a hotel banquet hall in Nippori.

I had my hair tied up, my lipstick matched the gaudy pink suit I'd been issued, and I was serving food and drink to a bunch of middle-aged men. I wondered if they, too, had fallen in love, married, started families. I was standing in a corner of the hall, staring into space, when Yabujika, one of the more experienced hostesses, came over. She had her long hair done up in a fancy bun and looked very smart in her white trouser suit with flashy gold buttons.

"What's up with you? Come on, get mingling."

"Right . . ."

"Your brooch is crooked." The tall Yabujika leaned down and adjusted the rose-shaped accessory pinned to my chest.

"Yabujika."

"What?"

"How do people fall in love?"

"What are you on about? Come on, you've got a job to do."

Dragging me by the arm, she reinserted me into the circle of middle-aged guys. Once they'd started getting nice and tipsy, I made my way over to the big bowl of salad, dished it out onto some plates, and walked around handing them out.

At dinner, I tried telling Ginko what had happened.

"So, you know my boyfriend . . ."

I didn't care what she thought of me, which made it feel like I could tell her anything. But now that I'd broken the silence of our meal, until then punctuated only by the clinking of plates and chopsticks, I began to regret my decision.

"He's been cheating on me."

"Oh?" replied Ginko, munching on a soy-simmered potato. Watching her, I started feeling like maybe this wasn't something worth bringing up after all, and quietly tucked into my own potatoes instead.

Everything Ginko cooked was bland and somehow unsatisfying. At my age, I craved food with a bit more substance. Cheese gratin, or barbecued meat, or carbonara – not thinly sliced daikon and dried fish.

"Is there any dessert today?"

"What?"

"A-ny des-sert to-day?"

"Nope."

"But . . . those apples . . ."

"Oh, them? They're not ready."

"Not ready?"

"They need to sit out overnight, or they won't taste any good, will they!"

When I'd emptied my rice bowl, I went over to look at the apples. Whenever Ginko had finished stewing something on the stove, she would always wrap a towel around the pot. She claimed that would keep the contents warm until the morning and help the flavour really sink in. The pot was swathed in an orange towel and filled with thin, limp-looking slices of apple. They were still warm, and glistened forlornly in the sugary water. They smelled good. I wondered about the girl who'd been sitting at Yohei's feet, and what her name might be. That dark, messy room of his seemed now to be pervaded, weirdly, by the sweet smell of the apples. Yohei really was an idiot, though. If it was sex he was after, he could easily have slept with any number of other people, so what had he been doing with me? And what on earth had I been doing with him for the past two and a half years?

I grabbed a slice of apple and gave it a good sniff. Some of it stuck to my nose, still faintly warm.

Ginko attended ballroom dancing sessions at the local community centre, and on Thursdays she would rush around, fussing over her make-up, before heading out. Of course, she took her smock off for the occasion. I suppose this was the sort of adorable behaviour people would normally coo over, but I just tutted to myself. What exactly was she trying to achieve by going ballroom dancing at that age, I wondered.

She kept insisting that I come along and watch, that it

would be fun, so every now and then, summoning up all the goodness I could muster, I would turn up and watch Ginko disappear into the throng of dancers with some old man. As the smartly dressed pensioners swayed back and forth around me, I just stood there, unsure what to do with myself.

With the break-up and everything, I felt like I needed a new start, so I got a haircut. I had it cropped short so that I looked like some fleet-footed primary school kid, and adopted a tough-looking expression to match. I decided it would be fun to surprise Ginko by bursting into the kitchen and shouting *rah!* But when I did, I found an old man I didn't recognise drinking a glass of green tea. He gave a little yelp of surprise, then started full-on choking.

"Sorry," I mumbled. While I was floundering about, trying to avoid his gaze and continuing to mutter my apologies, Ginko walked in.

"Oh, you've had a haircut!"

"Yeah. Um, I think I gave him a fright," I said, gesturing towards the old man, who was still spluttering.

"Oh dear. What have you done to Hosuke?"

"I thought it was you in here, but it turned out to be . . . someone else. Sorry."

"It's fine, don't worry," said 'Hosuke', a smile twitching across his face. Ginko was gently patting him on the back.

"Um, I'm really sorry." I slipped out of the room. Were they friends, dance partners, or was this some kind of silver-haired romance? I went to wash my feet, by now clammy with sweat, and was cutting my nails on the veranda, watching the trains pass, when I heard them leaving the house. I stuck my headphones on and started shaking my head all over the place. Then I closed my eyes and tried waggling my hands around too. It felt pretty novel being able to thrash my head around like that without my hair getting ruffled. Just as I was starting to feel a little dizzy, I felt my hand slap into something, and opened my eyes to find Ginko's thin legs right next to me. I looked up and there she was, standing there with a perplexed look on her face.

"What are you doing?"

"Oh, you know, just . . ."

Ginko stood there on the veranda, looking over at the station platform.

"Has the old guy gone home?"

"He's on his way now. Look, here he comes."

Ginko waved. The old man was standing on the platform, waving back at her. I straightened myself up and bowed. It's like gazing across the River Styx, I thought to myself, my vision still unsteady.

The two of them waved at each other for an absurdly long time. It was so drawn out that I started worrying they might have gone fully senile.

In the garden, weeds were pushing right up against the veranda. Specks of brown earth were visible amid the green, like mint-chocolate-chip ice cream.

SUMMER

≡ ◆ ≡

By now I was used to my three shifts a week as a host-ess and found myself wanting more work. As June came round, I found another part-time job, this time at a kiosk on the platform at Sasazuka station, a few stops from Ginko's place. I got them to give me around five shifts a week.

I worked mornings, six to eleven. The older woman who was showing me the ropes had started getting back pains and planned to quit once she'd trained me up. She was quite a talker. I followed her around, chipping in with little affirmative noises, asking questions, grasping this or that point, and generally feeling bored. At least twice a day she would lecture me about how everything would be a lot harder on my own and I should learn the job properly while I had the chance. I didn't tell her anything about where I was living or why I'd taken the job. I just wanted to get the hang of things quickly, so that she'd leave me on my own.

Getting up early was tough, but I got used to it. Mornings were the best time of day in the summer. When I left home at five thirty the sky would already be light, the air fresh, and there would be almost no-one waiting for the train. I would whistle to myself as I skipped down to the end of the platform.

In early summer the world's colours were bright and simple, like one of the drawings in the Miffy books. Every day, the weather was a carbon copy of the day before. People started dressing in more colourful clothing, and even the salarymen bustling around would take their jackets off, revealing bright white or blue shirts, so that the platform at rush hour was a flood of colour. It was enough to make your head spin. I loved the feeling that we were cramming in all the warmth we could before the rainy season set in. Little by little, I started remembering what it felt like to have sweat on my brow, or for my socks and underwear to get all hot and sticky.

The kiosk was right in the middle of the platform, facing away from the cluster of skyscrapers that was Shinjuku. I sold newspapers, chewing gum and bottled tea to a steady stream of customers. My memory was sharp enough that I'd soon learned the prices of most of the items thrust in front of me, and I was a handy shelf-stocker too. Even the apron I had to wear looked pretty good on me. I'd gaze at the middle-aged guy who bought the same bottled tea at the same time every day, or all the women hastily adjusting their make-up while they waited for the train, and think to myself: so this is the working world.

I learned to recognise the various station employees too. Mr Ichijo, who seemed to be the one in charge, would stand at the end of the platform every morning, and had a particular way of wearing his hat that somehow conveyed authority. Right from my first day, he had been considerate towards me and my lack of experience, and even now he never failed to say hello. He was middle-aged, but there was always something dapper and lively about him. Joining him on the platform were some younger part-timers.

Once, Ginko came to see me on the job. It was the quiet period just after the morning rush. I was gazing at Mr Ichijo at the end of the platform, wondering what he'd have been like as a father, when she appeared out of nowhere.

"Ginko! What are you doing here?"

"Thought I'd come."

"But . . . why?"

"Quite the working woman, aren't you!"

"Oh yeah. Just look at me go."

Ginko bought a couple of magazines, then walked down the platform stairs before reappearing on the platform opposite. I came out of the kiosk and waved to her.

Her train pulled in, and I waved again as it moved off with her on board.

When I got home from work later that day, Ginko was brushing the cats in the kitchen. Despite the sweltering heat, she was still wearing a smock, except now it was a summery pale blue. Judging from the pair of cut-glass tumblers and plates in the sink, the old guy had dropped by again while I was out. The plates were smeared with what looked like sweet soybean flour. They must have been eating warabi-mochi or something.

I grabbed an ice lolly from the fridge and sat on a chair with one knee tucked up while I ate it. When I'd finished, I turned to Ginko.

"So, you're in love?"

"Love?"

"Yep. You know, love."

Ginko grinned at me. "Have you fallen for someone, Chizu?"

"I'm not talking about me."

"If you say so."

"Seriously! I meant you."

"Oh, don't be silly."

"I just don't get what it's all about."

She just chuckled at that.

"Ginko, is there someone in your life you just can't forget, no matter how many years go by?"

"Someone I can't forget?"

"Go on, tell me."

Ginko finally gave in to my pestering and, still smiling, began to talk. She had picked up the brush, now covered in cat hair, and was fanning herself with it.

It turned out that, a long time ago, she'd had a romance with a Taiwanese man. She told me the story of her youthful, thwarted love.

"He was a good man, kind, tall, with these big round eyes. He'd come over from Taiwan, but his Japanese was excellent. We wanted to marry, but everyone opposed the match, and before I knew it he'd disappeared back to his own country. I couldn't stop crying. You know, raging against the world. I think I used up a lifetime's worth of anger back then."

"A lifetime's worth?"

"Yes. I don't really get worked up about things any-more."

"But how did you manage to use it all up?"

"I don't remember."

"I feel like maybe I should use up all my sadness now, while I'm young. So I don't end up all miserable when I'm old."

"No, Chizu, you can't go using it all up now. If you try and save all the fun for later, you'll be my age before you know it, and dying will seem like a pretty grim prospect."

"Is that how it feels to you?"

"Oh, you bet. Pain, suffering – that stuff's always scary, no matter how long you've been around."

I looked at Ginko waving the cat brush around as she said these words, and tried to imagine her heartbroken, crying, full of resentment towards the world. I couldn't quite picture it.

I hadn't felt truly sad or angry about anything yet, not really. So I had no way of knowing what those emotions would feel like as memories, either. On some vague level, I'd assumed that dealing with that kind of thing would come later.

I'd have liked to stay young, to lead a quiet life sheltered from all the drama of the world. But it seemed that wasn't an option. I was braced for my fair share of hardship. I wanted to try being an ordinary person, living an ordinary life. I wanted to become as thick-skinned as possible, to turn myself into someone who could survive anything.

I didn't know what dreams I was supposed to have for the future, or what people meant when they talked about meeting the love of their life. But those were the kind of things I found myself vaguely longing for.

Ginko really did seem to be in love with the old guy.

She had started wearing make-up and a pink lipstick that suited her light skin, and her hair was always done up nicely. She'd finally given up the smock, and instead started wearing short-sleeved floral dresses. I had no idea what the trends were among women her age, but she seemed to be making a real effort. Even when she stayed at home all day, she still took care to primp herself up.

With the onset of the rainy season, my own mood had taken a turn for the worse, and I became even ruder and grouchier than usual. I'd openly stare at Ginko while she groomed herself, saying nothing until she finally noticed and, a questioning look on her face, returned my gaze.

"Why go to all that trouble? It's not like there's anyone to look at you."

"Nothing wrong with making myself pretty, is there?"

"You do look pretty, I'll give you that."

"Oh yes . . ."

Sometimes the level of spitefulness I was capable of surprised even me. I would deliberately slouch around in my camisole and hotpants, showing off my firm, well-toned skin, though in the end it didn't make me feel particularly superior. For some reason, the more Ginko made an effort, the more my own mood soured. I wanted to do everything I could to thwart her attempts at being beautiful.

She must have noticed how I felt, because she started doing her beauty routine when I was asleep or out of the house. I would walk into the living room and there she'd be sitting, all dolled up already, drinking a coffee or something like she'd always looked that way.

"Very young at heart, aren't you, Ginko?"

"Me?"

"Yeah. Way more than me. I wish I could feel that young."

Ginko looked at me with a vaguely indignant expression, as if to say: what on earth are you talking about? She seemed to have realised I was making fun of her. I felt guilty, and yet I became even more sadistic.

"What's with that Hosuke guy, anyway. Is he your dance partner?"

"Yes. My dance partner."

"That guy *dances*? But he's all . . . shabby-looking. And his hair's a mess."

"Well, he's a good dancer."

"Great. Two singletons taking each other by the hands like that – I'm very happy for you."

"Hosuke is a kind man, you know."

"Really? He wasn't very friendly to me."

"He's just old-fashioned. You youngsters can be a bit overwhelming."

"Me, overwhelming? Huh. So I am still young . . ."

Whatever the age gap, we were still both women. Our gazes collided, laced with a strange blend of hostility and solidarity.

There was a scratching at the screen door. Ginko got to her feet and said, "Ah, I'll fetch a towel." I slid the door open and let the sopping wet Kurojima, who had been sharpening his claws on it, into the room. As I wiped the cat with the towel that Ginko had chucked in my direction, the raindrops falling on the veranda spattered against my knees.

*

When I woke the next morning I felt brand new. My body felt heavy under the clammy sheets, but I was brimming with optimism. Ginko wasn't up yet. As I sat quietly on the veranda nibbling on a bread roll, I became even more convinced that today would be a fresh start. After three gloomy weeks, the rainy season had passed. That morning, I had awoken to the real heat of summer.

As I was feeding the crumbs from my roll to a sparrow, Ginko appeared and gently prodded my bum. She was wearing a floral negligee and still had her curlers in.

"Morning!"

"Seriously? What's with the girly nightie?"

Ginko chuckled and disappeared off to the kitchen. One of her curlers came loose and plopped onto the tatami. I picked it up and tried to hurl it at the train platform, but it just hovered feebly in the air before landing a few paces away from the veranda.

Whenever I headed into town, it felt like my body, free from anyone's caress, was being somehow cleansed. I would close my eyes in the crowds and feel like I alone had become invisible, like everyone was passing through me. My fingers and hair were beautiful only for me. The trees lining the streets were turning a brilliant green, the air growing dense, people happily shedding their layers. When, after my bath, I applied a light cream to my body, I found myself longing for someone else to enjoy the fragrance.

And so the days went by until, on one of them, I fell in love.

He worked on the platform at Sasazuka station. He was one of the part-time attendants whose job it was to squeeze people onto Keio Line trains before they departed. In his tight-fitting white short-sleeve shirt, he was gallant, tall, rugged. His hair in a bowl cut. Light-skinned, his shoulders slightly sloping. He had a habit of taking off his hat with one hand, smoothing his hair quickly with the other, and then putting the hat back on.

When we happened to walk past each other, I snuck a glance at his badge and learned his name: Fujita. Just before the train doors closed, he would hold up a hand, rattle off some confirmatory phrase and glance past my kiosk. The idea that our eyes might meet gave me a private thrill. Once, when they really did meet and I nodded at him, he flashed me back an effortless smile.

I started fussing over my make-up in the mornings and trying to improve my posture when I was at work. At a quarter past nine, when the morning rush had subsided, Fujita and the other young part-timers would walk off down the stairs behind my kiosk, their job done. Until then, I spent every spare moment I had gazing at him in wonder. Watching him moving up and down the platform, cramming office workers onto the trains, I would think to myself: I am in love.

※

"Don't you think the station attendants look a bit like soldiers? You know, from some past era?"

"Not in the slightest," replied Ginko, breaking up a block of chilled tofu with her chopsticks.

"The hats, the uniforms – they're just so cool."

Ginko remained silent.

"I mean, tall guys look *really* good in those tight-fitting white shirts."

"Is that so?"

"Yeah, with the hats. And the white gloves. It's a great look."

Silence again.

Sometimes, when I sat opposite her eating dinner, I'd feel like I'd suddenly aged dramatically. When someone has been alive that long it can feel like they've stopped ageing entirely and it's just you catching up with them, hurtling through the years until you achieve the same level of decrepitude. She'd be picking away at the flesh of a dried mackerel, or peeling the skin of a summer orange, and I'd find myself suddenly overwhelmed by impatience.

"There's a new supermarket," Ginko said out of nowhere while we were eating dessert. I had an adzuki lolly in each hand and was taking bites from them in turn. On the television they were doing a make-up class for middle-aged or older women. A female teacher with glowing skin was making a bunch of ageing ladies look prettier.

"What?"

"They're building a new supermarket on the other side of the station."

"Oh yeah?"

"Fancy going?"

"When does it open?"

"Week after next."

"Sure. As long as no-one has died from heatstroke by then . . . Oh, sorry. I meant me, not you."

"I'm not sure I'll make it that long either!"

"It is *hot*, isn't it?"

I studied the middle-aged woman on the screen. She had bags under her eyes, thin eyebrows and faded wrinkly lips. A face layered with age. The teacher was using her slender fingers to restore colour to that face, bringing out its lustre, firming up its features. It was like the woman had come back from somewhere while also getting further away. At the end, she stood underneath a bright white spotlight and smiled. Everyone gave her a round of applause. Now that they were beautiful, the women on the screen looked content.

"Ginko, fancy looking like that? Want me to give you a makeover?"

"I think I'll pass."

"It's all fake, anyway, isn't it. Everyone clapping like that. I feel sorry for them. They look like a circus troupe."

Ginko pressed an adzuki lolly to her thin lips and smiled faintly. That good-natured smile of hers always triggered my spite.

"Hey, that old guy hasn't been round lately, has he?"

"Do you mean Hosuke?"

"Yep."

"No, he hasn't."

"Oh dear."

"I think he's just busy."

"Hmm."

Trouble in paradise, then. I felt weirdly pleased. When she saw the satisfied look on my face, Ginko raised an eyebrow, her eyes widening. Then she pulled a funny face. "What's with the face?" I asked, unable to stop a smile rising to my lips.

But, starting the next day, Hosuke began dropping by regularly again.

Having raised the subject just the day before, I couldn't quite believe this turn of events, and felt a little defensive. He started coming over for dinner a few times a week, too. To anyone else we would probably have looked like two grandparents and their granddaughter sitting peacefully around the dining table. Before I knew it, Ginko had even bought a pair of jet-black chopsticks just for Hosuke to use.

"Chizu, the three of us should go to Kotoya together sometime."

"Kotoya?"

"They do good food. It's near my station," Hosuke chipped in, actually looking me in the eyes for a change. But I turned back to Ginko.

"You two go there a lot, then? What kind of place is it?"

"They do Western food. It's really tasty."

"Right."

"Isn't that right, Hosuke?"

"Yes."

"So, what do you two, like . . . do together?"

"Oh, this and that. Eating together, going to our dance class."

Ginko didn't seem to have picked up on my mocking tone, and carried on munching away at her kinpira with a fixed expression. Hosuke, meanwhile, seemed to be ignoring me again. He had a vacant sort of look in his eyes.

The six o'clock news was still on the television. Whenever Hosuke came over we ate dinner ridiculously early, and we'd always get through two bottles of beer. As I watched him picking at the food with his chopsticks, I imagined his usual night at home, nibbling at ready meals and drinking alone, and began to feel a little sorry for him.

Hosuke lived three stops away, and when we'd finished playing happy families he would take the train home. Ginko and I would stand on the veranda and see him off. I didn't feel any particular affection for Hosuke, but when the three of us were all waving at each other like that, some of the usual venom seemed to leave my body, and that felt good. When he got onto his train and disappeared from view, the two of us would go back to our lives. Ginko would wash the dishes, and I would run the bath, and a slight tiredness would line our faces.

My daily three-hour sessions of gazing dreamily at Fujita continued. In order to focus on my work at the kiosk in the mornings, I'd stopped taking shifts as a hostess. Between six and a quarter past nine, when he was on duty, I'd be all full of life. The rest of the time, things were a little tough.

Lying on my futon at night, I would tell myself that tomorrow would be the day something finally happened, and as I fantasised grow wider and wider awake. I'd try to distract myself by focusing on the insects chirping incessantly outside, but they just reminded me of the cicadas in the daytime, and soon an image of Sasazuka station would have formed again in my mind. No matter how I tossed and turned, every inch of my sheets felt unpleasantly warm against my skin.

One night, I went to the kitchen to get some water, looked at the clock and saw that it was already two in the morning. Thinking I'd cool myself down a bit before returning to my futon, I quietly slid open the door to Ginko's room. Hers was the only one with air conditioning; apparently she'd had it fitted after a bad case of dehydration. She'd told me that if I got too hot I could always come to her room.

The air conditioning was on, and her room was nice

and cool. I stood there on the spot blinking until my eyes got used to the dark. The two cats were curled up by Ginko's feet. Tiptoeing past her futon, I made my way over to the glass cabinet, slid the door open and, taking care not to knock anything over, slowly inserted an arm. My hand landed on the Russian dolls, cool and smooth to the touch. I grabbed the outermost doll's head and pulled the whole set out in a single, decisive movement. Then, clutching them to my chest, I returned to the kitchen.

Without turning the light on, I took the dolls apart and lined them up one by one on the kitchen table. There were seven of them in total. The smallest was about the size of my thumbnail, and in the gloom of the kitchen I couldn't make out its face, or anything really. As I turned it over between my fingers, I once again found myself thinking of Sasazuka station and Fujita. I grinned stupidly to myself as I recalled, in detail, the way he stood on the platform, or his habit of scratching his head. After a while, though, I started to feel something like emptiness instead.

Telling myself that none of this meant anything, and that tomorrow would be just the same as today, I put the dolls back together again. When I'd finished, I sat there for a while, my head propped on one hand, staring at the tap above the sink.

The development I'd been waiting for came unexpectedly quickly.

There was an altercation at the kiosk, though I wasn't really involved. It was just after the worst of the morning rush had subsided. A couple came over to the kiosk arguing loudly with each other. "Just shut up, alright," said the man, as he held out a hand with a stick of chewing gum and some change in it, and that was the moment the woman, who was built like a sumo wrestler, chose to smack him square in the head. It took me a moment to register what was happening. Reeling from the blow, the man crashed into the products lined up along the right-hand side of the shop, sending them scattering across the platform, then angrily grabbed the woman's shoulder like he was about to punch her back. Mr Ichijo and a few of the nearby attendants came dashing over, asking what was going on. Fujita was among them.

Mr Ichijo got the woman to stop shrieking, and soon everything had calmed down. The man spat and said, "That bloody woman," like he was in a soap opera, then got on a departing train. The woman was helped into a lift and disappeared.

The young attendants were picking up the various products on the floor and putting them back where they belonged. Fujita was standing right next to me. I held out the stick of chewing gum that was still in my hand.

"Want this?"

"Are you even allowed to give me that?" he replied coolly. His voice was mellow and soothing.

"It's fine," I said, and thrust the gum into the pit of

his stomach. His white shirt looked like it was made of high-quality fabric. There were two thin lines on his breast pocket, so subtle you could only see them from up close. Seeing his badge with FUJITA on it only a foot or so away, my body practically seized up.

"Go on, take it."

"Alright then."

Fujita took the gum from my outstretched hand and slipped it into his breast pocket.

"I can give you something else next time, you know. Like, whatever you want," I jabbered.

"If you say so," he said with a laugh, then returned to where he'd been standing. My hands trembled as I restored order to the shelves. Sitting on the stool behind the counter and gazing at his distant figure from behind, I felt my body slowly unknotting itself.

At a quarter past nine, the part-time attendants walked off down the stairs together as usual. Except for Fujita, who, after he'd walked past the kiosk, turned back to look at me. When I summoned up my courage and waved, he raised his hand slightly at chest level to return the greeting.

A week later, we arranged to meet after work. He was the one who suggested it. I had watched him disappear down the stairs at nine fifteen, but at nine fifty, when I was least expecting it, he abruptly reappeared in front of the kiosk.

"When do you finish?"

"Eleven."

"Want to get some tea or something afterwards?"

"Yes."

"Okay. See you downstairs then."

"Right. Downstairs. Got it."

He nodded and walked off again. I watched him leave, then immediately looked up at the mirror in the corner. I started combing my hand through my hair even though it wasn't that messy and, though I knew it wouldn't help matters, squeezed a pimple on my right cheek.

That day, we went back to his place, a twenty-minute walk from Sasazuka station, but we didn't sleep together. I just had some tea with him and then went home. On the way there, I wiped my brow so many times that by the time we arrived my handkerchief was soaking wet. The make-up I'd carefully redone in the station bathroom seemed to have vanished.

He took a teacup from the cupboard, washed it, and brewed me some loose-leaf black tea. Even that left me dazzled, since I only ever drank powdered lemon tea at home.

The two of us sat side by side in front of the television until Fujita's flatmate came home, watching the lunchtime news and chatting about this and that. He'd put the fan on, but it was too close to me and my whole body felt sluggish. I sat there clasping my knees, sweat trickling between my thighs and calves, sliding my hand in between them and then gently pulling it out again.

❋

We started meeting up after work.

Fujita looked pretty good out of his uniform too. Today he was waiting for me in front of the bookshop by the station's south exit, by a small rest area whose other attractions included a lottery ticket booth, an ice-cream stall and a florist's – in other words, a fun sort of place all round.

We sat on the edge of a bed of azaleas, drinking soft drinks. There was a small hole in the right-hand sleeve of Fujita's T-shirt. The hairs on his nape formed a series of neat, inward-pointing rows.

With work out of the way, I had nothing else to do that day. I liked that feeling of blankness. I wondered if Fujita felt the same.

"What'd you want to do today?"

"Don't mind."

"How about meeting the old lady?"

"Old lady?"

"The one I live with."

"Okay, sure."

Ginko was out in the garden when we arrived. She was squatting by the hedge, pulling up weeds. For a terrifying moment, I thought she might be urinating.

"Ginko!" I called from the veranda. She looked over, wiping the sweat from her brow. When she spotted Fujita behind me, she came doddering over.

"We have a visitor."

They looked at each other. I took a step back and did the introductions.

"This is Fujita. And . . . this is Ginko."

"Hi. Thanks for having me."

"Hello there. Thanks for looking after Chizu."

"Oh, sure."

"Can I get you some tea?"

We sat there drinking cold green tea and watching *Omoikkiri Terebi*, a lunchtime talk show that had just started. It turned out that when you put three people with no conversation skills in the same place, all it did was ramp up the awkwardness of the ensuing silence. Just as they were finishing the part of the show called "Today's The Day", Ginko got to her feet.

"I think I'll make some chilled udon."

"Okay," I said.

"Will that be alright?"

"Oh, sure," replied Fujita, like he couldn't care less.

At two o'clock, Ginko went off to her dance class. She was wearing an old-fashioned white hat with a wide brim, sunglasses, and gloves to protect her hands from the sun. Fujita and I stood on the veranda and waved to her on the platform.

"Nice ageing film-star look she has going on there, don't you think?" I said.

"Good for her, I say."

"She's been really dolling herself up recently."

"Why's that?"

"I think she's in love. This wrinkly old guy from her dance class. She acts like she's our age."

I waved at her again, but Ginko's gaze was tilted upwards. She seemed to be observing something we couldn't see – the roof of the house, an electricity line, or maybe just the sky.

"I'm sleepy," said Fujita with a yawn.

"Want to lie down?"

"Yeah, let's."

Checking Ginko wasn't looking at the veranda, I shyly took his hand and led him to my room. Fujita looked quizzically up at the row of cat photos lining the walls.

"What are *those*?"

"The old lady's collection."

"It's like a headmaster's office or something in here."

"She calls them all Cherokee."

"Huh?"

"Once they're dead, she gives them all the same name. Cherokee. Pretty damn weird, right?"

I was beginning to think this would never work, not in this room. But soon enough we climbed under the sheets together.

Having sex for the first time in a while was awkward. I kept having to remind myself how it all worked. When he took off his clothes, his body was the same pale colour all over. The cats on the wall looked on. After we'd finished, I felt a wave of embarrassment.

When I woke, it was six in the evening. I rolled out of

the damp futon and lay there spread-eagled. During the lulls between trains, I could hear the sound of cooking in the kitchen. I manoeuvred myself over to the window and watched the colours in the garden changing as the sun set. Whenever a train went past, the mingled smell of concrete and vegetation seemed to intensify.

"Rise and shine."

I returned to the futon and laid a hand on Fujita's back. It was warm and sticky, and as I stroked it my hand grew damp with his sweat. I gave him a sharp pat and he opened his eyes, a morose look on his face.

"What time is it?"

"Six. Are you sticking around for dinner?"

"No thanks."

"Aren't you hungry?"

"Well, yeah."

"Then eat something before you go. Ginko will love it."

We threw on the clothes we'd cast off earlier. We both had severe bed hair. We washed our hands and went to the kitchen, where we found Ginko frying potatoes, carrots and meat in a pot.

"Ooh. Nikujaga stew?"

"It's curry, actually. Young people love curry, don't they?"

"Can't say I'm mad for it. How about you?" I turned to find Fujita scratching the back of his neck furiously.

"Sure, I like curry."

"Can we help cook?"

"No, I'm fine. Why don't you two have some tea or something?"

"Okay then. Let's go watch the trains."

I poured us some cold barley tea, then grabbed Fujita by the wrist and led him to the veranda.

"Not bad, right? I get to watch the trains all day long."

"Doesn't the noise bother you?"

"I'm used to it now. Anyway, it's good to have a bit of noise in a house like this. It'd be kind of depressing if it was just me and the old lady sitting around in silence."

"That street leads to the station, right? Couldn't you just cut a hole in the hedge so you can get through to it?"

"Yeah, I guess . . ."

Fujita took a cigarette from his pocket, stretched out on the veranda and lit it.

"What made you want to work at the station?" I asked.

"I like them."

"You like stations?"

"Yeah. All the hustle and bustle."

"The hustle and bustle, huh. Is that all?"

"I guess. There's no real reason."

"Do you enjoy the job?"

"It's alright, I guess. It's not like I expected it to be particularly fun."

The lights of an express train approached down the tracks, then sped past. There were only a few people dotting the carriages. The windows of the house rattled.

"I'm hungry," said Fujita, and downed the rest of his barley tea.

Ginko's curry was on the spicy side. Unlike all the other bland dishes she turned out, it packed a real punch. I had to keep swigging water. Spicy food wasn't my forte, and soon my eyes were weeping.

Fujita went home straight after dinner. Just as I'd asked him to do on the doorstep, he walked right to the end of the platform and waved goodbye to me. It was a parting that suggested there would be many more evenings like this to come. As I waved back, I felt a pleasant warmth spreading from the soles of my feet upwards. Even Ginko, waving away at my side, felt strangely precious to me.

The next day, I came back from Fujita's place to find a yellow balloon floating in the entrance. It had a rabbit drawn on it.

"What's this?" I asked, bringing the balloon with me into the living room. Ginko had her reading glasses on, a magazine open in front of her. She appeared to be dozing slightly, and her glasses had slipped to an odd angle.

"Hey. What's with the balloon?"

"Oh, that . . . They've opened that new supermarket. I went along to have a look and someone gave me it."

"It's finally open, huh. Well, this is fun."

Dragging the balloon with me, I walked barefoot from the veranda into the garden and started jogging around.

I stumbled on a flowerpot, gave an exaggerated yelp and tumbled straight into a patch of weeds. I wanted to be dashing around some rolling meadow, not this cramped little garden.

I decided I'd be a bit nicer to Ginko.

"Want me to do the shopping?" I called out, still sprawled on the ground, and heard something that sounded like a reply. "What was that?"

"I said it's okay, I've been already."

I went into a bridge pose, so that Ginko, standing on the veranda with her hands on her hips, appeared upside down.

"You'll get your clothes dirty."

"You didn't forget anything at the shop?"

"Nope."

"Fine then!"

She seemed impervious to my sudden niceness. I'd stopped caring anyway. I lay down again and, gazing upwards, wiggled the balloon around in the air.

"The cats are buried somewhere around there, you know."

"Seriously?"

I sat up and saw Ginko gesturing to where I'd been lying and tracing a circle in the air with her fingers. With a sigh, I moved to another patch and settled back down on the grass.

I could almost hear my sprawled arms and feet burning in the blazing sun. I let go of the balloon's string.

Closing my eyes, I felt an ant or something crawling along my left arm. I decided to let it keep tickling me.

Mum came back to Japan for the Obon holiday.

We heard a shrill "Hello!" from the front of the house, and then there she was, poking her face around the corner of the veranda. Ginko knew she was coming, but she still called out "Oh my!" and acted all surprised. I just glanced over and said, "Hi."

"Sorry for just showing up like this!" She left her suitcase in the garden, took off her shoes and came inside, plonking herself down where we had been quietly eating shaved ice a moment ago.

"Phew, it is *hot*," she said, pouting like a teenager. I offered her some of the shaved ice and she started whooping with delight. Ginko silently set about making tea.

"Thanks for looking after Chizu!"

"Oh, she's no trouble at all. She helps out around the place. Even cleans the bath every day!"

"Seriously? This slacker?"

Apparently she had been secretly sending Ginko money. Ginko had asked me to get her to stop, but I hadn't done so yet. I figured that if she was happy to send the money, Ginko might as well take it.

They talked to each other like two strangers. They kept interrupting each other by accident and then saying things like, "Sorry?" and, "What was that?" For some reason, the awkwardness seemed to have infected me and Ginko, too. There was even something overly polite about the way she handed me my tea. Meanwhile, Mum and I might be mother and daughter, but it was taking some time for us to readjust to each other's presence.

In other words, things soon became very stilted, and it wasn't long before my mum said we should get going.

She'd booked a hotel in Shinjuku, where we stayed for the next three days. Our room on the fourteenth floor had a view of Tokyo Tower, but not of my personal favourite, the Metropolitan Government Building. There was a flat swathe of greenery down below that must have been Shinjuku Gyoen, the old imperial gardens. I was still pretty clueless about Tokyo. All I knew was Ginko's neighbourhood, Sasazuka station, and the convention centres and hotel banquet rooms where I'd worked as a hostess.

With its crisp white sheets and spotless sink and toilet, our room had a pleasing sterility. It reminded me of an industrial clean room, a world apart from Ginko's creaking house full of cat hairs and red mould. If only I could have stayed here on my own, I thought.

We went to an all-you-can-eat cake buffet in the hotel lounge. There were cheesecakes, chocolate-dipped strawberries, Bavarian creams, fruit scones and an array of ice-cream flavours, as well as a team of suave male waiters arranging them on plates for us.

Mum had lined up eight flavours of ice cream alongside her plate of cakes and was gleefully working her way through them. She had changed her haircut, opting for a weird ringlet-style perm in what was presumably an attempt at looking youthful. I prepared myself for the inevitable moment when she would make me finish her ice cream for her.

"You've grown up a bit, haven't you?" she said, like I was some distant relative. Then she launched into a series of unnecessary comments – things along the lines of *You should smile more*, or, *Keep this up and you'll end up even more miserable-looking*, or, *Do you even have any friends?* Before long, she had reduced me to silence. It seemed that, the older I got, the less I had to say back to her.

"Life's going okay, then?"

"Yep."

"You studying?"

"No. Why would I be studying?"

"You've gained weight."

"Yep."

She, on the other hand, seemed thinner, her face sterner.

"How's China? Fun?"

"Well, it's very stimulating."

"*Ni hao.*"

"You're saying it wrong." She repeated it with what was apparently the correct pronunciation.

The other people at the buffet were almost all women, and they never seemed to stop talking. How did they manage to keep chatting away like that, I wondered? We were mother and daughter, and yet we had nothing in common to talk about, no old stories to make us laugh, no conversation we could lose ourselves in.

"We could have just stayed at Ginko's place."

"It's her house. We can't *both* impose like that."

"Then why didn't you just stay at the hotel on your own? It's a waste of money bringing me along."

"I thought you might enjoy a bit of luxury for a change."

"But I had to pack clothes and everything."

Mum looked suspiciously at me. It was an expression I remembered almost fondly.

"So you're not going to university."

"Nope. Bit late for that!"

"You still have time, you know. You've been slacking around long enough – don't you think it's time you actually *did* something?"

"Here we go again . . ."

"What do you even do all day? Just wander around?"

"No. I have jobs."

"What jobs?"

"Banquets. And a kiosk."

"What?"

"I'm a banquet hostess, and I work at a kiosk at a station. Sasazuka station. Heard of it?"

She gave a sort of sigh in response.

"It's nothing dodgy, Mum. I'm earning a hundred thousand yen a month."

I immediately regretted my attempt to impress her. In front of my mum, everything I had or owned felt somehow trivial.

"Chizu, you really should go to university. You'll end up wishing you had when you're older, and it'll be too late."

"But what's the point in going if I'm not interested? It'd just be a waste of money. I don't need a degree, Mum. I'll work something out."

"Well, yes, maybe. But . . ."

"You know what? I don't want to study. I want to work. I want to make my own way in life."

"Which is precisely why you should go to university. You know, some people seem to think you're desperate to go and the only reason you can't is because I'm a single mother . . ." Watching her sulk like that, I couldn't help bursting out laughing.

"As if anyone still thinks like that!"

"People do talk, Chizu."

"Who cares what I do, as long as we're both okay with it? I don't get why you're making such a fuss. It's not like you really care, anyway. You're just saying what you think a parent should say."

"Why do you always have to be so cynical?"

Plunging her spoon into her ice cream, now all but liquid, she gave me a prolonged stare. I tried staring right back at her, but my own gaze seemed to curl up and shrivel in front of hers like a newspaper catching fire.

"How can I put this . . ." Given how much effort she'd put into that glare of hers, she seemed to be struggling for words. "Do whatever you like, but do things *properly*, okay?"

"Oh, sure." I nodded, and got up to make my way over to the dim sum corner.

Doing things properly. What did that even mean? Going to university, working at some company my whole life? I doubt Mum herself even knew what she meant, but the very vagueness of the phrase seemed somehow to get to the heart of things, and it bothered me. Speak for yourself, I wanted to tell her.

Standing in front of a dim sum basket billowing with white steam, I turned around and looked over at her. She was slouched across a sofa that was practically swallowing her, swinging her legs from side to side, watching me. Flustered, I turned back around, grabbed the tongs, and filled my plate with a quantity of dumplings I knew I'd never finish.

That night, I slept with a pocket towel that Fujita had left in my room draped over my pillow. It had the stale odour of his sweat.

"What's that?" asked Mum, her expression unreadable behind the green face mask she had applied.

"It helps me relax."

"You know, when you were little you had a towel you always carried around, too. With koalas on it."

"Every kid does that kind of thing," I replied bluntly, irritated by her insistence on telling me about things I didn't even remember.

"Well, someone's in a mood!"

There was an unpleasant silence. We seemed to be growing further and further apart. I considered apologising, but I couldn't think of a reason to. I pulled my cover right over my head, hiding her from view.

How many years had it been since we'd slept in the same room? After switching off the light, neither of us said a word. I tried sifting through my memories with Mum for all the times I'd actually had fun with her. Sewing together on rainy days, late-night drives, picnics on the balcony – that kind of thing.

But those sorts of memories seemed only to scratch the surface. Instead, I soon found myself thinking about money, which came to me with a sharpness completely lacking from my hazy childhood memories. How much had she spent on me since birth – all the school expenses, the meals, the clothing, the travel? When would I ever be able to repay such an enormous sum? A heaviness filled my chest. Until I'd paid it all back, what right did I even have to criticise her? More than grateful to her, I felt beholden.

The same blood might run through our veins, but that didn't make us the same person inside. Ever since I was a teenager, I'd disliked my mum's affected youthfulness, that chummy tone she always took with me. The problem wasn't that she didn't understand me, but that she understood me too much. I suppose she'd worried that things might get claustrophobic with just the two of us at home, and decided she'd try to act like a friend who just happened to be my mum. But, whether from exhaustion or worrying about what other people thought of us, she'd never quite pulled it off, and I found that failure embarrassing.

I could tell from her breathing that she still wasn't asleep. The two of us were lying there, wide awake, as though locked in a silent contest.

On the afternoon of the second day, we went shopping together. In a way, it was fun. Mum bought me a cute pair of sandals, with a white dove on the left foot and a leaf design on the right. After dinner, she took me to the bar on the top floor of the hotel. That came as a surprise. I had no idea she went to such places.

We ordered cocktails with pretty colours. I glanced sideways at her as she gazed out at the night-time cityscape, and noticed that she was wearing more make-up than usual. Age had marked her features in subtly different ways to Ginko's, and as I looked at her I told myself I wanted nothing to do with it.

"You look older than you used to," I said.

"Well, having kids does take its toll," she murmured back, a hint of resignation in her voice.

"What, are you saying it's my fault?"

75

She didn't reply.

Through the window, the neon lights of Shinjuku station's east exit glowed garishly. We were there too, our reflections side-by-side in the glass. In outline, we had the same rounded cheeks. My mum seemed tired and somehow bored, and I felt like I might be to blame.

"I bet you just want to get back already, don't you?"

"Back where?" she replied half-heartedly, her cheek resting on her hand so that her nails dug into it. The varnish on them was peeling off, and they looked terrible. She had never painted her nails when we lived together. If she was going to bother, I wished she'd at least make a proper job of it. There always seemed to be a gap between how she wanted me to see her and how she really came across. But then I guess I never quite matched up to the image she had of her daughter either.

"China."

"Nope."

"So you'd rather be back in Japan?"

"Not really."

"What? Which is it then?"

"They're both . . ."

"Not where you want to be?"

"No, they're both . . . fine."

Mum was forty-seven, but she was still on the pretty side, at least from a distance. I wondered if she had a boyfriend or anything. I wondered if she felt lonely sometimes.

On the day of her return to China, we went to a

cinema near the east exit of Shinjuku station. The film wasn't great, which, combined with the glaring midsummer sun and crowded streets, put her in a bad mood. On the way to the station, she bought a hamper of fancy fruit from Shinjuku Takano and told me to take it to Ginko. When I said it was like she was making an offering to the dead, she got even moodier.

Striding off on the other side of the ticket gates, the handle of her big suitcase in one hand, she looked like a real, grown-up woman, a perfect stranger. She had neatly repainted her nails, though I had no idea when she had found the time. I'd only noticed them when we were saying goodbye and, with a smile, she stuck out a hand for me to shake.

I hadn't told her about Fujita, no matter how much she quizzed me about my life. It was probably just the kind of thing she wanted to hear. But if he left me one day, I'd have to tell her about that too, and that was a prospect I couldn't bear. It didn't bother me in the slightest if she thought I was naïve or full of myself. What I wanted to avoid was her pity.

I invited Fujita over to Ginko's, and the three of us had dinner together for the first time in a while.

"Your mother's gone back, then?" asked Ginko, dishing out the rice.

"She's meeting up with one of her old teacher friends in Ginza first. Her plane is tonight."

"Ginza. That's nice."

"Ginko, don't you ever go to places like Sugamo or Ueno? People say they're like Shinjuku for old ladies."

"I don't like the crowds."

"We should go together sometime. Fujita, you'll come too, right?"

I looked at Fujita, sipping his miso soup. That was the end of the conversation. Our meals together were always quiet and peaceful, like the unruffled surface of a lake.

All of a sudden, the weather cooled. Summer was ending.

Ginko, Hosuke, Fujita and I were setting off fireworks in the garden. Fujita and I held a bunch of them in each of our hands and danced around like crazy. The older couple set off one each and left it at that. When we ran out of things to ignite, everyone calmed down and sat on the veranda with their drinks. I went to get more beers from the kitchen. Hosuke's satchel was lying on the table, its zip open, the contents spilling out. I had a look through them but didn't find much of interest. There was a good-luck charm with his keys dangling from it, a wrinkled handkerchief, a black wallet, a paperback wrapped in a protective cover, some Jintan mints, and two sweets. I decided it had to be the mints, and slipped the entire packet into my pocket.

Back on the veranda, the three of them were gazing out at the garden in silence. If it wasn't for me, I realised, they'd probably sit here like this forever, unconcerned by each other's thoughts.

"More beer, anyone?"

Fujita grabbed the bottle from me and topped his glass up. I filled my own to the brim, then walked off into the garden.

I looked up and saw the moon, high in the sky. I sighed and stretched out contentedly. My beer spilled onto my arm.

"Summer's almost over," I said, and turned around to find three pairs of eyes staring at me. I burst out laughing, which only made the whole situation feel even funnier. I seemed to be the only one enjoying myself.

Fujita sprawled out on the veranda and started tapping away at his phone. Hosuke was getting ready to go home, with Ginko helping him.

As well as the chirping of cicadas, I could hear some other insect singing, one I didn't recognise. Maybe it was a cricket of some kind – a korogi maybe, or a suzumushi. I didn't really know the difference.

AUTUMN

═══◆═══

I was accompanying Hosuke and Ginko on one of their dinner dates. I hadn't been too keen on the idea.

"You know, I think I'll just stay here."

"Don't be like that. We need a youngster around sometimes. When it's just us oldies staring at each other, we can get a bit . . ."

"Sick of each other?"

"Oh, not that. We're not like young people, Chizu. Our feelings don't come in waves."

We were meeting Hosuke at his station. Ginko and I walked to the end of the platform and looked across at our house. Under the white glare of the streetlights, the one-storey building looked small and shabby. The only impressive tree in the garden, the sweet olive, wasn't in flower yet.

"Looks sort of sad, doesn't it? With the lights off, you wouldn't think anyone lived there."

"I suppose."

"But we do live there."

"Oh yes."

"Do you like it there?"

"Well, I've been there long enough. So yes, you could say I'm attached to the place. By the way, did you let the cats in?"

"Yep. Both of them. Brought them in with the laundry."

Our train pulled in, and Ginko tottered slightly in the dry rush of wind.

Hosuke was waiting at the ticket gates. The two of them walked off, discussing a typhoon that was on the way. I followed behind, my hands in my back pockets. Even now that we'd entered the second half of September, it was still hot during the day, and I'd come out in short sleeves. But the evening wind carried a chill.

Hosuke's station was just as dreary-looking as ours. The road that ran parallel to the platform was lined with star-shaped streetlights, but they were old and grimy and didn't give off much light. Glancing through the windows of a supermarket by the station, I saw that the staff and customers were all wearing strangely vacant expressions. Maybe Ginko would go on to Hosuke's house after dinner, and I would ride the train home alone with a similar look on my face.

Kotoya, the restaurant they were both so keen on, was above a soba place, down a side street that ran alongside the supermarket. The stairs must have signalled danger to my elderly companions, because they ascended them with great care. Ginko grasped the railing with her right hand and the sleeve of Hosuke's thin sweater with her left.

It was still early, and the restaurant was empty. The woman running the place must have been in her early fifties. She greeted Hosuke warmly.

"Oh my – is this your granddaughter?"

"No, actually," replied the old man firmly.

"More like a friend of a friend," I chimed in, straightening my posture as I spoke.

Without acknowledging what I'd said, the woman started explaining the menu. Seeing as it was Hosuke treating us and I was feeling a little rebellious, I decided I'd really stuff myself. I ended up drinking five glasses of expensive-sounding plum wine too. Ginko ordered a glass of shochu that supposedly tasted like chocolate wheat puffs. I tried a sip, but all it did was make my mouth burn.

While the two of them picked away at a single plate of cabbage rolls, I silently devoured everything I'd ordered: beef tendon braised in black vinegar, veal Milanese, German potato salad, mackerel sushi wrapped in bamboo leaves, and an orange sorbet. When the woman was clearing away the empty plates, she smiled and commented that I had a youthful appetite. "Oh yes, I'm very youthful," I replied.

Hosuke saw us to the station. We said goodnight and

went our separate ways. From the platform, Ginko and I watched him disappear off down a side street.

"You're not going to his place then?"

"Oh no. Not at this time of night."

The station clock showed twenty past eight.

"That's normal, is it?"

"What?"

"You know, when people your age are dating."

"Oh, I'd say it depends on the person."

"Don't you ever go to a hotel or something? There's one down the main road, you know. With a big duck by the entrance. You should go somewhere fancy like that."

"No thanks." Ginko smiled slightly. She had three big wrinkles running across her brow, and deep hollows under her eyes. Between her nose and mouth ran another long wrinkle that looked like it could easily hold a pencil. When she smiled, they all became more pronounced. I felt strangely guilty and looked away.

Later that evening, it started to rain. The typhoon was coming. The wind picked up, and soon the shutters were flapping about loudly like they were about to fly off.

In the middle of the night, I started feeling unwell, and before long I was regurgitating everything I'd eaten earlier. As if spurred on by the fierce winds outside, I started making over-the-top retching sounds. Soon they developed into a weird rhythm. Tears and snot ran down my face, mixing with the vomit.

It must have been the mackerel or something. I was laid up in bed for two days. For some reason, Ginko escaped unscathed.

Autumn was here, and Fujita and I were still seeing each other.

There were no ups and downs with Fujita, no sudden bouts of niceness or nastiness. We really are quite similar, I thought. I started feeling like maybe I was in a proper, happy relationship, just like all the other couples I saw in the streets.

We would meet up after work, have lunch at Ginko's, and then laze around together. I tried never to look at him too intently, and when I touched him, to be as brusque as possible, never too tender.

One day, I stole some of his cigarettes. He was dozing in my room, and I took a whole pack from the pocket of the battered jeans he had taken off. He smoked menthol Hopes. Apparently he liked the green colour.

"You seen my cigs?" he asked when he woke up.

"No. Can't you find them?"

"No."

"Maybe you dropped them somewhere?"

I wondered if he knew. He didn't say anything. I was sitting by the window, staring at him. For a moment, his expression was sullen, but when I told him to join me, he wrapped his naked body in the duvet and crawled over. We watched a few trains go by.

"Do you feel that rush of wind when they pass?" I said.

"Oh yeah?"

"Sometimes, I get super jealous of the people riding the trains. You know, the fact that they have somewhere to go. The furthest I ever seem to get is Sasazuka."

"But you could go anywhere you want. Just get on a train."

"Yeah, I guess . . . How about going somewhere together, then?"

"Like where?"

"The mountains."

"The mountains?"

"You know, Mount Takao or something."

"But we'd get all hot."

"True. I mean, we'd be closer to the sun and everything . . ."

He didn't reply to that.

On the narrow road on the other side of the hedge, some schoolkids with little yellow caps on were making a racket, yelling to each other about it being a dead end. One of them started shaking the hedge, and soon the others joined in. Their little chubby hands kept appearing and disappearing between its green leaves.

"Reckon they're trying to get through?"

"Yeah. Like I said, you should cut a path through. It'd make it quicker to get to the station."

"Well, yeah, but . . ."

"Come on, let's do it."

Fujita sat up and reached towards his pile of clothes by the futon.

"But," I said, a little startled. "The hedge has been like that for so long. Ginko might have some special reason for keeping it that way. I'm not sure we should—"

"Chi, you're always over-thinking things."

There was an edge in his voice that had never been there before, one that reminded me of my own voice when I was nasty to Ginko. It sent a chill down my spine.

"That's not true."

Fujita just looked at me.

"You're just as bad, anyway," I added, flustered.

He stretched out lazily, then wrapped himself in the cover again and turned his attention back to the hedge. The kids seemed to have given up on trying to get through and were galloping off towards the station. After a moment's silence, I pulled myself together and said, in my usual carefree voice:

"You staying for dinner?"

"Sure."

"Good. You should just live here, anyway. You know, move out of your apartment."

He silently pinched my thigh. It was almost sunset.

After that, I started taking Fujita's other possessions when he wasn't looking.

He didn't carry much around with him, so instead I'd take stuff from his apartment: a toy car that had come free with a can of coffee, a keychain, a thick finger ring, a pair of boxer shorts. I'd take them home with me, study them carefully, then put them in the shoebox. Whenever I did, I'd take the other objects out and, as if honouring the memory of the dead, recall their former owners.

The cap that the most popular boy in my year wore to gym class. A flower-patterned eraser from the girl who used to sit in front of me. A red pen belonging to the maths teacher I'd fancied. A piece of junk mail addressed to our neighbour that had been mistakenly shoved into our letterbox.

I retrieved a crumpled ball of tissue and opened it up to reveal a short human hair. It was Yohei's. I'd cut it from his head while he was sleeping. It was jet-black and curly and completely different from Fujita's. When I pulled it at both ends, it split soundlessly in the middle.

I held the box up close and sniffed it.

With the passing years, the objects inside had slowly faded away, gradually losing their individual smells and colours. I wondered if I'd changed with them.

"Ginko, do you think I'm more mature than when I started living here?"

"More mature? Not really. Anyway, you've only been here half a year or so, haven't you?"

"What? You mean I haven't changed at all?"

"Well, with someone your age, it's hard for an old lady like me to tell the difference."

"Oh, you old ladies all seem the same to me, too. Do

you even, like, remember how old you are? I forget my own age sometimes . . ."

"My age? I can remember that much, yes."

"How old are you then?"

"Seventy-one."

"Do you feel young for your age? Or just right?"

"Oh, I feel young . . ."

"Huh. Really . . ."

I'd be twenty-one next year. The old lady had been around half a century longer than me. It seemed unlikely I'd ever learn the story of those fifty years.

Fujita and I went on our trip to Mount Takao.

The autumn leaves weren't quite at their peak yet, which meant it wasn't too crowded. We climbed the mountain, enjoyed the fresh air, had a bowl of yamakake soba by the station and went home again. I spent almost the entire hike staring at the ground in front of me, while Fujita hurried wordlessly to the summit. I could barely keep up with him.

"Can we slow down a bit?" I'd asked him, gasping for breath. For a moment he just looked curiously at me. Then he said, "Sorry," and took my hand.

On the train home we stretched out our legs, our matching trainers sticking into the aisle, and nibbled on Pocky sticks. Every now and then, we'd exchange a few words.

While we were waiting for an express train to pass

ours at Tsutsujigaoka station, we heard what sounded like a collision, and then a series of dull thuds as the express ground to a halt. The other passengers on our train began muttering and getting to their feet.

We got off the train and saw station attendants rushing across the platform. They were climbing down onto the tracks and peering under one of the carriages. The express train had stopped just after passing the platform. Almost all the passengers from our train had disembarked and were staring silently at the scene.

"Looks like we'll be here a while," Fujita said. He didn't seem very concerned by what was happening.

"Oh, god. Did someone jump in front of the train? Have you seen this happen before?"

"No, not personally."

"You think they're dead?"

"I guess so."

I had the urge to go over to where the station attendants were gathered. I wanted to see what a dead person looked like.

"Let's walk home," Fujita said, tugging my sleeve. Holding his hand, I was relieved to find it as warm as ever.

Near the stairs leading to the ticket gates, I noticed something that resembled a maple leaf on the platform. With my poor eyesight it was hard to tell, but it seemed to be a bloodstain, or maybe a sliver of flesh.

When I pointed it out, Fujita stopped short and

murmured, "Woah." It was some time before I could tear my eyes away from the red spot.

"Pretty horrible way to choose to go, don't you think?" I said.

"Chi, I'm not planning on dying, full stop."

"Clock's always ticking, though, isn't it?"

"Come off it. We've got ages."

"But, I mean . . . you never know, right? You might just be sitting there one day, and then all of a sudden, poof, you're dead."

"So what?"

There wasn't much I could say back to that.

Just like Hosuke, Fujita now had his own pair of chopsticks at Ginko's house, although his were sky blue.

He no longer seemed especially happy to see me at the station. So why were we even still together? I didn't want to admit it, but I seemed to be falling into my old pattern. Sometimes the way Fujita treated me reminded me of Yohei: the tone of his voice when I interrupted him reading, or the way he never matched his pace to mine.

His uniform had switched to a brown suit with the arrival of autumn, but my eyes were still glued to him as he went about his duties or stood there watching the trains pulling in and out. Even when he stretched his feet out at home and revealed his dirty toenails, or shot me one of his annoyed looks, I found myself wishing things between us would last.

*

"Um, Ginko," I said, lingering deliberately on the *um*. "Do you think you could stop using my toner?"

Ginko raised her eyebrows and opened her eyes wide. "What's that?"

"It's for young people, anyway. I don't think it works on old ladies."

"Sorry, what are you talking about?"

"You know, my toner. The stuff by the sink. It's expensive, so could you not use it? I had a look just now and there's about *this* much less of it than there should be," I said, showing her a gap of about five centimetres between my thumb and forefinger. Some exaggeration was only called for.

"I haven't used *that* much," she mumbled. She really is going senile, I thought, but all I said was, "Right then." I made my way to the veranda and started trimming my nails.

Once I started laying into her it was hard to stop. Her frail, thin body and apparent inability to ever speak loudly made her the easiest of targets. If I really wanted to, I could probably have reduced her to tears.

Recently, though, I'd begun to suspect that Ginko was deliberately turning a blind eye to my simmering resentment. When she ignored my childish goading and played the innocent old lady like this, it only wound me up even more.

Still, I drew comfort from the knowledge that, physically at least, I had the upper hand. It was a feeling of confidence that seemed to be growing in inverse proportion to my dwindling faith in Fujita. But if it went unchecked, I realised, I'd only get more and more aggressive, and eventually Ginko might wither away completely. And so I would consciously swallow the cruel words that were on the tip of my tongue.

Whether I moved out, or Ginko died first, it wasn't like we had decades of this life together ahead of us. In the meantime, it would be best if we just got on. And when we did part ways, I wanted it to happen naturally, with as little fuss as possible.

There was a new girl working at the station.

The moment I saw her, I felt a rush of anxiety. Here we go, I told myself. She was brisk and efficient and seemed never to make any unnecessary movements. When our eyes met, she came all the way over to the kiosk to say hello.

"I'm Itoi. It's nice to meet you!"

The look in her eyes reminded me of a particularly friendly dog. Her dark brown hair was tied in a bun that stuck out from the back of her hat.

"Chizu. Nice to meet you."

She flashed me a smile, then went back to her post. Mr Ichijo was supervising her. She was pretty slim, and the brown trousers of her uniform looked baggy on her. Her shoulder pads seemed out of proportion with the rest of her. Watching, I felt anxious for her, like she might be swept away by the crowds. Her armband with the characters for "attendant" on it kept slipping down her sleeve.

At ten past nine, I saw Fujita go over to her and say something. Once I was sure the image had seared itself onto my retinas, I calmly closed my eyes. When I opened them, they'd gone their separate ways.

I went home alone that day. We'd been walking home from the station together less often recently. With extra time on my hands, I'd started taking hostess shifts again. Fujita, meanwhile, had started another job at a restaurant in Shinjuku in the evenings. Apparently the place specialised in Haitian food. I asked him why he'd decided to work there, but all he said was that someone had offered him the job. To me, Shinjuku felt about as far away as Haiti.

When I got home, I spotted Hosuke's leather shoes in the entrance and decided I'd carry on walking. I followed the nearby ring road all the way to the municipal pool, rented a costume and went for a long swim.

A group of older women were lined up in the water, doing walking exercises under the watchful eye of a middle-aged male teacher. On this autumn weekday I was the only young person there. I swam until my head started spinning, then rested by the pool. Lying on the bench, the scenery outside the window seemed unbearably vivid. There was a row of shrubs that had lost all their leaves, and on the other side I could see cars coming and going. A plastic bag got caught in a gust of wind and blew onto the windscreen of a car waiting at the lights. A cyclist had to swerve to avoid some pedestrians on the pavement.

I imagined Ginko and Hosuke back at the house, nibbling on little rakugan cakes or the like as they chatted away.

Itoi and I were the only girls working on the platform, and apparently that meant we had to be friends. She kept saying things to me, like "Warm, isn't it?", "Cold, isn't it?" or "I'm so sleepy."

Fujita always called her Ito-chan, so I started doing the same. The two of them would move together and apart on the platform as the waves of people came and went. Whenever I saw them getting closer to each other, my insides swirled, as if my stomach was being pulled at from both sides. I couldn't tear my eyes away from them. It was an addictive sort of agony.

Itoi tugged on Fujita's sleeve and said something. The two of them turned in my direction and gazed at me from a distance. I pretended not to notice and started restocking the chewing gum and sweets on the shelves.

At a quarter past nine, as the other part-time attendants were leaving for the day, she came over.

"How about getting lunch together today?"

"Um, today?"

"Yeah. With Fujita."

"Sure. I finish at eleven. Does that work?"

"I didn't know you two were a thing. He told me just now, when I mentioned how you were always looking over at us."

I gave a little chuckle in response, but on the inside I was less calm. A middle-aged guy was approaching the register with a can of coffee in his hand, so Itoi said, "See you later," and dashed off. "Uh-oh," I muttered under my breath. The middle-aged guy, who had just taken his change, said, "Sorry, what was that?"

When I finished work, I found the two of them waiting for me on a bench by the lottery ticket booth. They were sitting weirdly far apart, but it looked like the conversation was flowing. The area by the station had lost its summery sheen. The ice-cream shop had closed down, and the white-and-blue striped streamers hanging in front of it now looked weather-beaten and sad, like grubby old blankets.

Itoi's hair was around the same length as mine. We were both wearing Adidas trainers and carrying only a small handbag. Looking at her, I started to feel like some poorly turned-out copy. I wondered if the two of them had been sitting there chatting away like that for the whole hour and a half they'd been waiting for me, sounding each other out, growing closer and closer. I realised that I'd never really seen Fujita chatting to another girl. It had always just been the two of us. Ginko aside, I'd never even imagined what he was like around other people.

Sitting there with his legs crossed and a smile on his

face, he began to seem like a complete stranger. My legs felt wobbly. I wondered if I should just go home, but then they noticed me.

"Hey, Chizu!"

Itoi stood up and waved. She had a nice smile, the kind that cheered you up. I found myself smiling back at her.

At the restaurant, Fujita and I sat alongside each other. Itoi was opposite us, talkative, unassuming. Still, I felt incredibly uneasy. I tried mentally superimposing Ginko's wrinkly face on Itoi's, but that didn't help.

Fujita munched away at his fries next to me. Every now and then he would say something that made her laugh. Sitting there, laughing along with them, I began to feel like I was observing myself from behind. At the same time, it felt like someone else was watching me as I watched.

"Sorry, I should get going," I said, and got up.

"What, why?" asked Fujita, looking up at me, an annoyed expression on his face. Itoi looked concerned.

"I told the old lady I'd take her to the hospital. Sorry, but I really have to go."

I stuck a thousand-yen note on the table and headed back to the station. I found myself running so fast I got a stitch.

Standing on the platform, I looked up. The sky over Sasazuka was clear and blue. Then I looked down at the street in front of the station, at all the people coming and going below the rows of Zelkova trees, wondering if I might spot Fujita and Itoi among them.

When I got home, Ginko was making biscuits, rolling out the dough and carving it into shapes with a cutter.

"Ugh. What are you making those for?"

"I'm taking them to dance class. Some children are coming to watch."

"Children, huh? Well, don't mind if I do." I peeled a piece of dough that had been cut into a star off the table and put it in my mouth.

"Hey, I haven't baked that yet."

"I like it raw."

"You'll get sick."

"So, is Hosuke coming today? You two still getting on nicely?"

"Hosuke? Yes, I suppose." Ginko looked up and smiled at me, her hands still working away.

"Oh, right." I paused. "Well, it looks like it's over for me."

"What do you mean?"

"You know, with Fujita."

"What happened?"

"It's just over, okay. It always works out this way."

"Chizu, you shouldn't overthink things."

"Oh, I'm not overthinking anything. I can just tell."

"These things are never as bad as you think they are."

"But once I get it into my head that it's over, that's

usually what ends up happening. The idea just sort of grabs hold of me, even if I try not to let it."

"All we really are is the part that sticks out from the mould. That's the real you."

Ginko gathered up the leftover dough, rolled it out and cut it into shapes, then repeated the process. Soon the baking tray was packed with rows of star-shaped biscuits.

"So the real me is a pessimist?"

"There's nothing wrong with a bit of pessimism, Chizu."

"If I died, nobody would even care."

"That's not true."

"Everyone would prefer me to be all cheerful and pretty and sweet."

"Okay, these are ready to go in!"

Ginko put the baking tray in the oven, then started cleaning up, humming to herself as she did the washing-up. A small pink gift bag and some gold ribbon sat waiting for the biscuits at one end of the table.

"Ginko, are you even listening?"

"Oh, I'm listening."

"Well, I'm glad you're having so much fun. Already done all the hard stuff, haven't you? I bet every day is a real blast when there are whole decades you don't even remember."

"Are you not enjoying life then, Chizu?" asked Ginko, still facing the sink.

"Nope. Not even a little bit," I replied, but my words were drowned out by the sound of water rushing from the tap, and I don't think Ginko heard them.

Next they invited me ice skating.

I told them they should just go on their own, but Itoi wouldn't take no for an answer. I was finding her hard to read. Did she really just want to be my friend, or was she deliberately trying to hurt me?

"But it's still autumn."

"It gets crowded in winter."

"I've never even been ice skating."

"Oh, you'll be fine. We'll have you gliding around in no time."

"You reckon?"

"Don't worry, I'll teach you. Fujita knows how to skate too, so we can prop you up from either side."

Wondering how she knew that about him, I looked at Fujita, hovering behind her like some guardian spirit, and asked him if it was true.

"Oh, yeah," he replied breezily, with his arms folded and his shoulders all hunched up. Maybe he was cold. I watched them go off down the stairs together, then found myself gazing at my own hands. I couldn't wear gloves while I was working at the kiosk, and my knuckles were cracked and red from the cold.

After eating lunch together, the three of us made our way from Takadanobaba station to the ice rink, walking side by side. Itoi was wearing a green knitted hat and a red cardigan. She looked like Christmas on legs. Preferring to avoid Fujita, I stayed close to her, and we linked arms as we walked.

There was almost no-one else at the ice rink. The skates were heavy and uncomfortable. Watching some kids gliding around in colourful frilly clothes, I began to feel slightly more motivated. I want to do that, I thought. I managed to get onto the rink, but then found I couldn't let go of the barrier. Fujita clasped his hands behind his back and skated off, a composed look on his face. Itoi took my left hand and started eagerly giving me instructions. Once I'd made it all the way around the rink once, we leaned against the barrier and studied Fujita, gliding around with his scarf fluttering away.

"He's good, isn't he. Bit cruel, though."

"Yeah. Not very nice of him to abandon you."

"He's always like that. You know, I don't think he even likes me that much."

"Oh . . ."

Itoi made a pitying sort of face. I didn't want that expression of hers, which I'd apparently triggered, anywhere near me. Looking at it I began feeling like I really was someone to be pitied.

"It's okay, Ito-chan, you go skate. I'll be here, practising with the barrier."

"Oh no, I'll stay here with you!"

"I'll be fine. Go on."

"You sure?" Itoi made an even more uneasy face, then set off across the rink. When she caught up with Fujita, the two of them started skating side by side, like some happy young couple. Well, that looks fun, I found myself thinking as my own skates scraped across the ice.

Whenever Itoi skated past, she'd come over, say, "You okay?" and hold out a hand.

"Go on, try taking your hand off the side. You'll be fine, I promise!"

I gingerly did as she suggested, clinging desperately to her gloved hand.

"Hey, Fujita, come take her other hand."

Fujita did as he was told, and finally came over to my side.

Clutching their hands, I tottered forwards. I was just about managing to walk, but I couldn't work out how to push my heels out and skate. I lurched from left to right, unable to keep my balance, then leaned on Itoi so much that she shrieked.

"You're pulling my arm out of joint!"

Panicking, I tried to lean towards Fujita instead. Then, with a yelp, I stumbled, and the three of us fell onto our backsides. The tips of my toes were stinging inside my undersized skates. I wanted to go home. I wanted to be somewhere warm, drinking cocoa on my own.

Ginko's dance group were putting on a performance for Labour Thanksgiving Day. It was being held at the cultural centre, one station away from the house. I invited Fujita along.

The street leading to the venue was quiet, and dust swirled around us in the wind as we walked along in silence. I'd mentioned how cold it was when we left the house, but since then neither of us had said a word. I stopped in front of an estate agent's to look at the apartments on offer, but Fujita just carried on walking.

When we got there, the lobby was filled with a display of hand-drawn cards and calligraphy. A troupe of heavily made-up elderly ladies marched past with bright yellow garlands around their necks, leaving a trail of perfume in their wake.

The hall was small but new and well equipped, and almost all the seats were taken. On the stage, old ladies in white blouses were playing handbells with some primary-school age kids. When that finished, Ginko walked onto the stage in a frilly purple dress, together with another group of elderly people. Hosuke was there too, holding Ginko's hand, a bow tie around his neck. They made a pretty fetching couple. Ginko was wearing thick purple eyeshadow and stood there proudly on the stage.

When the music started, and the gentle dance began, I felt just the tiniest bit happy.

"Don't you think it's nice?"

"Sure," replied Fujita.

"I'd like to try dancing sometime."

He stayed quiet.

"If I did, would you be my partner?"

"No thanks."

I gripped Fujita's hand throughout the performance, as though trying to will him into not disappearing. He kept yawning and after a while fell asleep.

"So, I won't be coming over for a while."

We were sitting in my room after dinner. Here it comes, I thought.

I kept blowing away at my mug of kobu-cha, pretending I hadn't heard him.

"Chi, did you hear me?"

"Nope."

"You did, didn't you?"

Fujita snorted. The sound made me flinch. He seemed like a total stranger, someone to be afraid of.

"I said I won't be coming round here much." There was a pause. "So, yeah . . ."

"Why?"

"It's . . . various things."

"What does that mean?"

"You know, this and that."

He didn't seem to have anything else to add. He lit a cigarette. When he exhaled, he pursed his lips like a flautist.

"You're not going to come over anymore?"

"Yeah, I guess."

"You like someone else, don't you?"

"No, it's not like that."

"I know you do."

I put my hand on his arm, but he pulled away.

"It's Ito-chan, isn't it?"

"No. I mean, I don't know. Sorry."

"You might as well come out and say it."

I kept staring at him, but he averted his gaze.

"How can you be so casual about this?"

"About what?"

"About everything . . ."

"What's everything?"

"I don't know, okay?"

I didn't quite have the heart to blame Fujita for going off me. I hated the fact that he was leaving, but I had no idea how to stop him.

"Don't do this," I said. It was all I could manage.

He asked me to think it over and, apparently without doing much thinking himself, left.

I went into the living room to find Ginko watching a crime drama and knitting a scarf. It was orange, with a tight weave. I stood there leaning against the wall for a moment, watching her.

"Is that for me?"

"What?"

"The scarf. Is it for me?"

Ginko shook her head vaguely. Her glasses had slipped all the way down her nose.

Exasperated, I went back to my room. The window pane was rattling away. I sat by it and felt the cold draught against my skin. There was no sign of Fujita on the station platform.

The thought that this might have been his last visit made it hard for me to turn back around. I didn't want to have to touch the cushion he'd sat on, or the mug he'd drunk from. Maybe it would be best to simply forget the whole thing. I could just consign everything that had happened with Fujita to the far reaches of my memory, along with all the other boys. Strip him of all his distinguishing features and turn him into another "Cherokee", a dead cat to line the walls of my room.

I closed my eyes and asked myself if that was something I was capable of. But it seemed impossible. I didn't want Fujita to disappear like that, not yet.

At some point, I'd become deeply attached to him. Whether my lingering obsession was something to be happy about, or distraught, I didn't know.

I'd assumed that as long as I felt that strongly about Fujita, and patiently focused on those feelings every day, they would eventually make their mark. But apparently that wasn't how it worked.

I kept calling and messaging him, but he remained cold and distant, as if I was gradually vanishing from his world.

At Sasazuka station, he deliberately avoided my gaze.

Itoi was her usual chatty self, but I could only manage brisk phrases in return.

I tried his apartment in Sasazuka, but he always seemed to be out. The guy he lived with would look all sorry for me as he sent me on my way. Once, after he'd shut the door, I heard male voices laughing inside. One of them was Fujita's. I hadn't realised he was that desperate to avoid me. Now I really did feel hurt. I tried to clear my head by walking all the way home. It took me three hours, but in the end I just felt even more pathetic.

The following evening, he called to say he was coming over. Overjoyed, I redid my make-up and sat there waiting for him. He turned up with all the books and CDs he'd borrowed, as well as his spare key.

"Do you want to come in for some tea, or . . ."

Standing there on the doorstep, it took all my nerve just to say these words.

"No, I'm good. There's somewhere I have to be."

"Oh . . ."

He was acting so nonchalantly that I accidentally ended up following suit. Against my will, I seemed to have turned into the kind of person who understood these things. That look on his face, that distance he'd created that let me know it was all over without him having to say a word – where had he learned them?

"Shall I get Ginko?"

"No, don't bother."

"Don't you want to see her?"

"It's not like all three of us were in a relationship, is it?"

"Well, no, but . . ."

"You know, this house always makes me feel like I've suddenly aged."

I wanted to ask whether that was really so bad, but all I managed was a vague smile. It didn't seem like anything I said now would make a difference.

"Chi, by the way. You said how casual I was being about everything, but I don't think that's true. The thing is, you—"

"Fujita, just forget about it, okay."

I was standing on the step just inside the entrance, but Fujita was still taller. Normally, all I could see was his Adam's apple, but standing here I only had to look up slightly to meet his gaze. It was the same angle I'd seen him from whenever I'd greeted him or seen him off.

"Well, bye then," I said, unable to bear the silence I'd created. Not wanting our last moments together to be too depressing, I gave him a smile and a wave.

"Yeah, bye," he replied.

"I'm guessing you don't want me to contact you."

"Yeah, if you don't mind."

"Well, okay then."

Inside, I was screaming: *No, no, no!*

"Take care of yourself," I found myself saying idiotically as he walked off.

The door slid shut, and the sound of his footsteps

faded. I wanted to chase after him, but my feet wouldn't move.

Somewhere he had to be. Where could he have meant?

In the living room, Ginko was nursing a cup of tea in front of the television. I slid into the kotatsu opposite her and opened my eyes wide, in an expression that said, *Told you so*.

"What's with the face?" she asked.

I settled under the blanket and opened up a newspaper like everything was fine. I could feel Ginko staring, and it irritated me.

"Did you hear all that then?"

"Hear what?"

"I know you did."

Ginko did a little chuckle, which didn't seem very appropriate. Then she said, "People can be awful, can't they?"

I didn't say anything.

"Always upping and leaving," she continued, getting up to take the kettle off the stove.

A check flannel shirt was hanging on the chair in the kitchen. Fujita had left it here in early autumn, and now Ginko had got into the habit of wearing it when it was cold. She pointed at it.

"Oh, he forgot his shirt. What shall we do with it?"

Dozens of possible answers swirled around my head, but all that came out were the words "I don't know".

I curled up on my side, burrowing under the blanket

so that it was just my head sticking out. After a moment, Ginko's green knitted socks sidled into view, together with a miniature tub of Lady Borden ice cream which she placed in front of my nose together with a teaspoon.

"Go on, tuck in."

I pulled the blanket over me completely and started eating the ice cream.

That was when the tears came. Vanilla was Fujita's favourite flavour. He never even went near strawberry or chocolate. Whether or not she'd done it on purpose, I felt vaguely annoyed with Ginko for picking vanilla ice cream of all things. Then I found myself thinking that one day she would leave me too, and the fact that I didn't want her to, that an old lady like her had become the only person I could turn to, made me seem all the more pathetic.

It all seemed so hopeless. When would I stop feeling so alone, I wondered, and then flinched at my own thought. Was I really so scared of being on my own? It seemed like such a childish thing to be afraid of . . .

Kurojima was curled up under the corner of the kotatsu, snoozing away. I remembered Ginko telling me how, in the old days, the kotatsu was heated using a charcoal fire instead of an electric heater, and one of her cats had died under the blanket as a result. When I gently prodded his rounded back with my toes, he opened his eyes and, with an annoyed expression, shifted his body slightly.

I lay there in a ball, my face a few inches from Ginko's small feet in her green, heavily pilled socks. By now, I was crying less out of sadness and more at how pathetic I was.

I woke to the near terror of having absolutely no plans that day.

A chill ran down my neck. I closed my eyes and tried to sleep some more, but the morning light was blinding. I hid under my duvet and tried to swallow my fear like it was nothing, but it was hopeless. Two days after Fujita's last visit to the house, I had quit my job at the station.

I went to the kitchen. Something smelled good. When I realised it was curry, I started to really salivate. The sunlight pouring through the window over the sink made it hard to make out Ginko's silhouette as she stood there, facing away from me, stirring the pot. Where had all her sadness gone, I wondered. Her anger. Had she expelled them with words? Was it really possible to "use them up" like she claimed she had?

"What's that you're making?"

"Curry."

She didn't turn around. I stood next to her and stared at the boiling contents of the pot.

"Isn't it a little early for that?"

"Want some?"

"No."

"Oh."

"I told you before. Just because I'm young doesn't mean I like curry . . ."

It was an effort just to speak, and I found myself trailing off. Ginko scooped a small amount of rice onto a flat dish, then ladled over some curry, taking care to include a few chunks of vegetable.

"I'm going to boil that down a bit. Could you watch it for me?" she said, then disappeared off to the living room.

I quietly stirred the curry. I could hear the clink of Ginko's spoon from the other side of the sliding door. Gradually, my mind became quiet too, a flat surface. As I stirred, I imagined my sadness slowly dissolving into the pot of curry.

With nothing to do, I decided to walk to the library by the next station. On the way, I noticed some graffiti on the concrete columns supporting the elevated railway line. At the end of a long scrawl of blue spray-painted characters was the cheerful phrase *It's time to give up on life!*

Huh. Time to give up on life. Okay then.

Maybe it was some kind of cry for help. I pictured someone, probably younger than me, leading some angry, hate-filled existence, their every waking moment fraught with danger.

I wish that was me, I thought, as I walked along nibbling at some chocolate I'd bought from a convenience store. I made my way into a park whose paths were lined with gingko trees, quickening my pace now, kicking at piles of dead leaves as I walked. I passed a primary school where, on the other side of a sky-blue fence, children in short-sleeved shirts and shorts were running around and shrieking. When a teacher in a tracksuit blew a whistle, they abruptly fell silent.

I gripped the fence and pressed my face up against it as hard as I could, like some local deviant. I could make out the distinctive fragrance of the sweet olive trees. The children had formed ranks, and now yelled as, one by one, they set off running.

I wish I could just disappear, I thought.

I remembered the suicide on the tracks that I'd seen with Fujita. That bloodstain smeared across the platform, the colour of maple leaves. If I cut my own body, would the blood that flowed be the same bright red? Something told me it would be more like a murky brown ooze.

I felt somehow exhausted. Exhausted by my own endless inner monologues, by the blue of the sky, no longer what it had been in the summer, by the thin legs of the children, by this boring walk down this boring path, and by the life with the old lady who was waiting at the end of it.

A gust of dry wind blew my hair onto my face. It had grown a lot since I'd had it cut in the spring. The season was changing, along with my body and all the other things that didn't matter to anyone.

WINTER

≡ ◆ ≡

Ginko's dress looked weird. The shoulders were all wrong, the ribbon waistband was way too low, and the whole thing was strangely baggy, like she was wearing a coat underneath. She looked like a teruteru-bozu, one of the ghostlike paper dolls people hang in the window to pray for good weather, except it had sprouted legs.

"What's with the outfit?" I asked coldly.

"It's a maternity dress," she replied, leaving me speechless. She's finally lost it completely, I thought.

"Planning on getting pregnant?"

Ginko chuckled. "Oh, I wish!"

"Too late for you."

"I suppose."

"Anyway, kids only end up letting their parents down."

"You can't know that until you've had one."

"Then I guess you should ask Hosuke to help you out."

Hosuke was still coming round often enough. I'd stolen three packets of Jintan mints from him by this point. Twelve of his sweets, too. That was all he had for me to take. You'd think he would have noticed by now – or maybe he had and, being Hosuke, just wasn't saying anything.

"Why does love always fade, Ginko? And why hasn't yours?"

"Must be the wisdom of old age, I suppose."

"That's so unfair. You oldies get all the luck. What have young people got to be happy about?"

"Chizu, you should fall in love lots while you're young."

"But it all seems so meaningless."

Every evening, I would get out the things I'd taken from Fujita and gaze at them. I tried smoking one of the cigarettes I'd pinched from him, but it was damp and tasted bad.

The weeds in the garden had all wilted. The cats had stopped going outside too. Instead they just curled up in front of the kerosene heater with me.

"When are you two planning on dying, eh?"

When I tugged on their whiskers, Kurojima and Cha-iro looked irritated and went off to the kitchen. The dessert plate on the low table was piled with mikan oranges.

I had nobody to chase after, and all anyone ever seemed to do was leave me. So what was this feeling of impatience in my chest?

I wanted to pound madly on the keys of a piano. Burn all the clothes in my drawers. Toss all my jewellery from the top of some tall building. Smoke ten cigarettes at once.

Maybe that way I'd be able to shake myself free.

I felt like I'd never be able to lead a normal existence. Everything that came into my grasp I threw away, or else it was snatched from me, while anything I actually wanted to be rid of remained stubbornly by my side. That was all life seemed to consist of.

I had stopped taking shifts at my evening job, and found myself spending more time with Ginko.

When I crawled out of bed at eleven in the morning, I found her drinking a cup of tea, sewing needle in hand. Apparently her latest thing was embroidering blue flowers onto handkerchiefs. She'd gone round the house finding all her handkerchiefs and now she was furiously stitching away.

That night I'd dreamed I was skating with Fujita. I was still just as unable to take my hand off the barrier, and just as frustrated with him for not bothering to help me. Even when I lost it and started yelling his name like a little kid, he still wouldn't come over. For some reason the skating rink was next to Mount Takao, which I started climbing with my ice skates on. The people at the ice rink were shouting at me, telling me to come back, but the louder their voices grew the more stubborn

I became, scrambling frantically up the narrow mountain path.

When I woke up my legs felt like lead. Without washing my hands or doing my usual morning gargle, I grabbed a teacup, pulled the kotatsu blanket over me and got Ginko to pour me some tea.

"I feel like there's no point in being alive," I muttered.

"No . . . point?"

"Yes, Ginko," I went on, my voice dropping to a barely audible whisper. "I just can't see the point."

She didn't reply.

I thought of Fujita. Him, and all the other people I'd ever been close to. It unsettled me that my connections to others could be so flimsy. I seemed incapable of establishing a solid bond with anyone. I wanted to live on my own. Instead of other people always leaving me, I wanted, just once, to be the one to leave.

Was it time to move out?

I wanted to sever all my connections, to make a fresh start in a place where I knew nothing and nobody. But even then, I'd only end up forming new relationships, which sooner or later would themselves wither away. And if I let that process repeat itself over and over, without ever questioning what any of it meant, my own life would eventually come to an end. How many times had the old lady in front of me gone through exactly that cycle?

"I wish I could time-travel."

"What?"

"Like a time warp, until I'm your age."

"*Time warp?*" she asked, repeating the English words I'd used.

"Yeah. I'd skip forward a few decades and then I'd be all old like you."

"Don't be silly, Chizu. Your twenties are as good as it gets. Plus your skin's all nice and soft."

So she *had* noticed my skin. I guess I'd been showing it off enough.

"All old people seem to think that. I'm not sure being young is all it's cracked up to be, Ginko. Moping like this over every little thing – it's exhausting. I'm so sick of it."

"Oh, but you're just trying out all your options while you can. When you get to my age, they start to dwindle."

I kept catching glimpses of the blue flower on the piece of fabric she was embroidering. It had a yellow pistil. Her fingers were working away relentlessly.

"Is it easy being an old lady?"

She chuckled. "Is that how it looks to you?"

"Yep. I'm telling you, being young is a real downer."

"But you've had your fun moments, haven't you?"

"Nope."

"Come on. Try actually remembering."

"Even if I do, it's not like the fun itself is going to come rushing back."

"That's not true. If you do it right, it all comes back."

Ginko finished off her blue thread, then gently tugged at the part she had embroidered with her fingertips.

"What do you reckon?" She opened it out in front of her, her face looming faintly through the white fabric. It looked like one of those veils they put over people's faces when they die.

The hostess company was still calling me every now and then, so I got them to take me off their register. Then I found myself a new job at a company that sold and leased water coolers, doing admin work at their office in Ikebukuro. I was only a temp employee, but I plugged away from Monday to Friday, nine to five.

As I slid water cooler pamphlets into envelopes, running a finger down the list of customers and checking them off one by one, I tried to imagine the worst possible turn things might take in the future. A huge earthquake or fire, for example. A gas leak. Ginko dying. Mum dying. Running out of money. Running out of clothes. Losing my home. I had no friends, no partner and nowhere permanent to live. All I had to rely on was my own mind and body, and I wasn't even sure I could trust those. Still, it looked like I was going to have to make things work on my own.

When I was done, I looked at the resulting mountain of envelopes and felt pleased with my achievement. It was oddly satisfying, this feeling that I'd *done some work*.

In the pink waistcoat and grey skirt I'd been issued, I looked every bit the dowdy office lady, and the three o'clock snacks I was indulging in to reward myself for all this hard work meant I soon gained a few kilos. With the cold mornings, it took me a while to roll out of bed and I never had enough time to get ready. My make-up became increasingly slapdash, and I started wearing glasses instead of bothering with my contacts.

I felt myself becoming less and less attractive. This is a disaster, I would think bitterly as I looked in the mirror of the office bathroom.

A cold wind blew every day. When I finished work, I would bury myself in my scarf, hat and gloves and hurry home. As for the Christmas lights that annoyed me so much every year, I decided that the people who enjoyed them should just go ahead and enjoy them, and that was that.

Hosuke came over for Christmas, and the three of us had a little celebration. Actually, all we really did was eat a cake. Decorations or presents didn't seem to be a thing at Ginko's house. Hosuke turned up all nattily dressed, although he hadn't gone quite as overboard as he had for the dance performance. He'd wrapped a familiar-looking orange scarf over his tweed coat, combed his normally dishevelled white hair and even put on a tie. I looked at Ginko and realised she'd spruced herself up too and was wearing a tighter dress than usual. Feeling underdressed in my jeans and hanten jacket, I decided I'd go back to my room and smarten up.

As I stood there trying various clothes on in front of the mirror, I found myself gradually getting into the spirit, and even got my eyeliner out for the first time in a while. When I swept back into the living room, Ginko exclaimed, "Ooh, someone looks pretty!"

"You think?"

I was wearing the shiny beige dress I'd once worn to my cousin's wedding. I'd done my hair up and put on a pearl necklace too.

"Oh yes. Light colours like that really suit someone your age."

Hosuke was smiling at me too.

"Does it suit me?" I asked, doing a twirl in front of him.

"Oh, definitely."

"Thanks. Appreciate it."

The three of us sat there at the kotatsu in our fancy clothes and ate our meal as usual, before quietly tucking into a Christmas-themed sponge cake.

I wondered what Fujita was doing right now. He was probably having fun at some Christmas gathering with Itoi. They'd be wearing those conical party hats. It surprised even me how clearly I could visualise the scene. All of a sudden, the cream in my mouth tasted bitter.

"So, we're going on holiday," said Ginko, poking at her cake with a fork.

"Huh?"

"Hosuke and I. We're off on a trip. Fancy joining us?"

"Me? Where are you going?"

I still couldn't shake the image of Fujita and Itoi and their party hats from my mind.

"Onahama."

"Where's that?"

"It's a port town in Fukushima."

"Sounds freezing. I'm good, thanks. I'll keep an eye on this place instead."

"We're going in the new year. You've got time to think about it!"

"I've got work, anyway. You two should just go on your own."

In her way, Ginko seemed concerned about me. I guess she thought I was still reeling from the break-up.

The truth was, little by little, I was getting used to my situation. I'd been in it enough times in the past. However different Fujita had seemed from other boys, my slow and barely conscious recovery from apparent hopelessness felt depressingly similar.

As the year was coming to an end, Mum made another visit.

This time, she came through the front door like a normal person, wearing a white coat that she seemed a little old for. She looked well.

"Hey," she said, waving as she spotted me sitting at

the kotatsu, cutting up dried squid. "Look at you, you're a mess. A girl your age should make more of an effort!"

"I'm fine like this, actually."

I didn't have work that day and was still in my pyjamas. I hadn't even looked in the mirror yet. I reached a hand to my hair, which was getting longer and longer, and found that it had settled in a dramatic curl on one side. Saliva had dried around my mouth, and when I rubbed it with my nail, it pattered onto the table in white flakes. Ginko was in the kitchen, simmering dried anchovies to eat over the new year.

Mum had booked the hotel in Shinjuku again. Four nights including New Year's Eve, with her going back to China on the third. I didn't feel great about Ginko spending the new year alone, but I couldn't exactly leave Mum on her own either. She could have just stayed at Ginko's house, but she didn't seem to even view that as an option. I guess she still felt guilty about never staying there when she was younger.

Just like in the summer, we went to the cake buffet in the hotel lounge. I was dipping strawberries in the chocolate fountain. Soon, Mum joined in.

"This is fun, isn't it?"

"Yeah."

"So, anyway," she began, as she speared a fifth strawberry onto her skewer. "I might be getting married."

"What?" My hands froze.

"I said I might be getting married," she said calmly,

plunging her strawberries into the chocolate. Her expression implied this was nothing to get worked up about.

"To who?"

"Someone I met in China."

For some reason, I found myself thinking of my mum's nails when we'd met in the summer. I looked at them and saw that today, too, she had painted them a light beige. I realised I should say something.

"Well, congrats."

"Huh?"

"I mean, good for you."

"You think?"

"Well, it's not like you need to ask me for permission. Not at your age."

"Really? Well, alright then."

She put her strawberries on her plate, their red skins now smothered with chocolate, then moved on to a slice of melon, which she skewered and thrust in my direction. As I took it and dunked it in the chocolate, I tried to imagine her married to a Chinese man. All I could picture was her frying dumplings.

"So are you going to become Mizue Li, or Mizue Chou, or something?"

"Oh, I doubt it."

"Why?"

"Well, he's asked me to marry him, but I'm not sure I want to."

"Why not? What's stopping you?"

"Oh, this and that. Work's busy. I might marry him at some point, but not right now. So, did I give you a shock?"

"Not really. But Mum, if you keep stringing him along like this, he's bound to give up on you."

"Oh, I doubt it," she said with a chuckle. "Anyway, China isn't so bad, you know. There's all sorts to see. If you did want to come . . ."

"I think I'll stick with Japan, thanks."

"Suit yourself. Well, I guess we won't be seeing each other much, then."

"Yeah, guess so," I said, and laughed.

"You're fine with that, are you?"

Fine with what, I wondered. Something that might have been happiness or sadness welled up inside me, and I felt an urge to walk off and leave my mum right then and there. I decided to focus on the cascade of chocolate, but I could feel her peering expectantly at me. I had no choice but to turn back to her and say something.

"Yeah, I'm fine with it."

She seemed to be waiting for me to go on.

"I said I'm *fine* with it," I repeated, louder this time.

I picked up the plate of fruit and hurried back to my seat and started eating. Mum lingered by the chocolate fountain. Why had she mentioned getting remarried if she wasn't even going through with it? And should I have reacted differently?

Mum finally came back over, her plate packed with

brightly coloured cakes, then wordlessly deposited half of them in front of me, a satisfied look on her face. As she picked at her cakes with a fork, I could sense her glancing at me, trying to gauge my mood.

When we got back to our room, she handed me a fancily wrapped parcel. My Christmas present, apparently. Inside was a teddy bear.

"Thanks," I said, though I wasn't exactly thrilled. It was cute enough, but I wished she'd given me something that wouldn't take up so much space – a ring, maybe, or a necklace, or a hand mirror.

"What about my New Year's pocket money?" I asked, sticking out my hand, but she just pushed it to one side.

"Oh, come on. You're a grown-up now, aren't you?"

In that case, why had she given me a teddy bear? Still clutching it, I dug around in my bag and retrieved a small parcel, which I chucked onto her bed.

"What's that?"

"For you."

"Ooh . . ." She began unwrapping it excitedly. Watching her in the mirror, I prayed she wouldn't be disappointed.

"Oh, beautiful!"

She put the bracelet on straight away, then held up her wrist.

"Do you like it?"

"It's lovely. Thanks. You really have grown up, haven't you?"

"Oh yeah. Full-blown adult."

"Want to see Mr Wang's photo?"

"Who's Mr Wang?"

"You know, the guy who wants to marry me."

She extracted three photos from a notebook she had in her handbag. The first was of Mr Wang, the second of my mum and him, and in the third they were joined by a little girl. Mr Wang wore glasses and looked every inch the pleasant middle-aged guy.

"Who's the kid?" I asked, pointing at the girl in the photo. She was beaming away in my mum's embrace.

"That's Mr Wang's daughter. Her name's 'Keika' if you pronounce the characters the Japanese way."

"So he comes with a kid, huh?"

"She's cute. Says she wants to come to Japan."

I stared for a long time at the girl who might one day be my little sister. My little Chinese sister. I wondered if we'd teach each other our languages.

When I looked up, my mum was looking at me like it was her birthday and we were at her party. To me, it felt as though one of the threads connecting us had snapped. As she accumulated her own baggage, mine was gradually disappearing.

I handed the photo back to her and went over to the window. I'd been meaning to study my face in the reflection, but before long my gaze was drifting between the neon signs of Kabukicho.

✳

On New Year's Eve, I called Ginko. I thought I might as well say thank you for looking after me all year. I didn't bother ringing until ten in the evening, and she seemed to have gone to bed already. After the tenth ring I hung up. Maybe she'd gone over to Hosuke's place. In fact, I hoped she had.

"Hey, didn't Ginko ever remarry?"

"Oh, I have no idea."

Mum was sprawled out on the bed, doing her shaping-up exercises. She kept twisting her body around and bending her arms in weird directions.

"You think she's just been living there on her own since her husband died?"

"Well, when I went to see her right after I'd had you, she was living with some handsome man. I assumed she'd remarried, but later I found out that wasn't the case. Anyway, why don't you just ask her?"

"It feels a bit late for that now."

"I don't know her that well either, you know. I've never really spent any time with her. But she's a good person, don't you think?"

"Oh yeah, she's a good person, but . . ."

"But what?"

"She's a bit weird, isn't she?"

"You two are perfect for each other, then."

"I worry she might turn senile."

"Oh, she already has a bit, don't you think?"

"What? No, Mum. She's okay."

127

I guessed she might seem that way to anyone who wasn't living with her. But as far as I could see, for now, Ginko was doing just fine.

After the clock struck midnight, I called her again, but the phone just rang and rang. She must have gone to Hosuke's place after all. Still, just to be on the safe side, I sneaked off to the house on New Year's Day, praying along the way that she hadn't slipped in the bathroom or something.

When I opened the front door, the two cats emerged, mewling noisily. I wondered if Ginko had ever left them on their own for the night before. Cat food was heaped in their bowls and scattered nearby.

The navy-blue shoes she always wore weren't in their usual place by the entrance. Still, I did a sweep of all the rooms, calling out *Ginko-o-o?* as I went.

On the evening of the third of January, we saw each other for the first time that year.

"Happy New Year, Chizu. I hope it's a good one," Ginko said with a deep bow. I bowed back just as deeply. Beneath her smock, she was wearing that baggy dress of hers again.

"That looks comfy. Nice and warm, too, I bet?"

"Oh, this? Yes, isn't it nice?"

"So, how about my New Year's treat?" I asked, sticking my hand out a little optimistically. To my surprise, she produced one of the envelopes used to give kids money. On it was a picture of Miffy on a bicycle.

"Wow. Seriously?"

"Well, you've been good company this last year. Go on, take it!"

"Thanks. I didn't think you'd actually give me anything."

I peeked inside the envelope when Ginko got up to go and make tea. There was only a thousand yen inside.

I never told her that I'd tried phoning or come over to the house. If she wasn't going to tell me where she'd spent New Year's without me asking, that probably meant she didn't want me to know.

On my first day back at work in the new year, my boss summoned me to his office. His dark hair was streaked with grey. On his desk was one of the cheap mochi cake decorations they sell at supermarkets. I told him it was pretty, and we chatted a bit about how we had each spent the New Year, and then he went quiet for a moment. Then, dropping his voice for some reason, he asked me if I wanted to become a permanent employee.

"Me?"

"Yeah. We've got some vacancies opening up. And you seem to know what you're doing."

"You mean . . . I'd properly work here?"

"That's right. Think it over. I'm told there are spare rooms in the company dormitory too, so you could move in there if you wanted."

I told him I'd think about it. I didn't know what to do. Had the time finally come for me to settle down?

Since April, I'd been earning as much as I could, but I'd still only saved three hundred and fifty thousand yen. It would soon be a year since I'd moved to Tokyo, but I was way off my target of a million. Presumably I'd earn more as a permanent employee. It wasn't like I had any real plans for what to do with all that cash, but in terms of realistic goals, the concreteness of that figure – a million yen in savings – was all I had.

When I started seriously considering whether moving out of the house was something I'd be able to do, I found myself feeling guilty about Ginko. I guess I really did feel affection for her. It also felt wrong, somehow, to be moving out just when I was finally getting used to living with her.

"What's the company dormitory like?" I asked Ando, who I was having lunch with as usual. There was no cafeteria at the office, so we would buy bento boxes from the convenience store and eat them in the smoking room on the roof. When the weather was good, we'd go outside, but today it was so cold that we came right back in.

"The dormitory? Well, it's a single shot from here on the train, so that's convenient. You're coming all the way from Chofu at the moment, right?"

"That does sound easier . . ."

"Oh, definitely. It's cheap, too. And the rooms are nice enough."

"Cheap and nice, huh?"

"Why are you asking, anyway?"

"Oh, it's just . . ."

"Wait, are you being made permanent? That would make sense, with two people leaving this month and everything. Hey, good for you!"

"You'd recommend it, then?"

"Oh, definitely. I mean, think about the insurance. What are you going to do if you get sick?"

"What do you mean?"

Ando stopped tidying up the tray of pasta she'd just finished and turned to me with an incredulous look on her face. She had orange sauce around her lips.

"No insurance means you have to pay your own hospital bills, even when they're massive. Right?"

"Is that the only thing?" I asked, dabbing at my mouth with the tissue that came with my bento.

"I'm not really sure, but I think there must be other perks."

"Is it easier to save up cash when you're permanent?"

"Well, business isn't great at the moment, so I wouldn't get your hopes up. But if you live in the dormitory then yeah, you should manage to save a bit more."

Was I really going to blossom into a fully-fledged "office lady"? Pay my taxes, my pension, my insurance every month like a proper member of society?

"The office life, huh?"

Ando took a puff of her cigarette. "What, don't you fancy it?"

*

When the department stores started putting out Valentine's Day banners, Ginko mentioned that she wanted to buy some chocolates.

"Getting Hosuke a little something, are we?"

"That's right."

"Huh. Chocolates for grandpa. Nice."

"Will you come with me, Chizu? At my age I'm clueless about these things."

"And you think *I'm* not?"

"Oh, you youngsters always know what's what."

"I'd say an old person would probably know what's best for an old person . . ."

The following Sunday, we went to a department store in Shinjuku. Ginko was wearing a lilac two-piece dress and cream pumps, and her white hair was gathered into a bun at the nape of her neck. A compact little old lady. And, in her own way, pretty cute.

When the train stopped at Sasazuka station, I looked down at my feet. Whatever I might tell myself, I still couldn't bring myself to look across the platform. I didn't want to risk Fujita or Itoi seeing me. How long had it been since the three of us last met? I wondered if they even remembered my face.

The train pulled out of Sasazuka and went into a tunnel, and I finally looked up again. Ginko and I were reflected in the window opposite. There was Ginko, all dolled up, and fast asleep. Good on her for going out and buying chocolate at this age, I thought to myself. When the train briefly shuddered, she looked up in surprise, then closed her eyes again. "Sleepy?" I asked. She didn't reply.

Could I become an old lady like her one day? Dressing nattily right into my seventies, living in a little house all of my own, and going out to buy chocolates for Valentine's Day – was that a life I could live?

The top floor of the department store had a whole area called the Chocolate Centre. It was heaving with women. When we got out of the lift, Ginko suddenly came to a halt.

"My, what a crush."

"Come on, let's go. We've come all this way!"

"You go have a look. I'll be waiting over here."

"Seriously?"

"This is all a bit much for someone my age, Chizu."

She started looking at the pick-and-mix chocolates by the lift. For some reason, it was the only place that wasn't jam-packed. I began making my way through the crowd.

After trying a few samples, I hurried back over to Ginko, and was relieved to find her sitting on a chair next to the lift. This was what old people did, I thought to myself, they always managed to stake out a place of their own. When I said hello again, she patted me on the arm and said, "Oh, good work." There was no hardness or heaviness to that hand of hers, I thought, and yet somehow she had managed to come this far in life all by herself.

I took her over to a store near the entrance that had caught my eye.

"What about these? 'By appointment to the Viennese court', it says. Not bad, right?"

"Ooh. Yes, these look good. I'll get this one, I think. Look, it's a cat."

Ginko had already decided. Her finger was pointing at a sky-blue cat-shaped box containing an array of thin chocolates.

She started trying to give the salesgirl some money, so I tugged on her sleeve and showed her the separate cashier area. There was a long line of women at the tills, each clutching their own small box. We stood there and waited for our turn, queuing in weary silence.

I had already decided to move out.

I need to tell her soon, I thought, as I stood behind her gazing down at the whorls of her hair. But how was I going to break it to her?

"Ginko."

Thwack, thwack, thwack. She was chopping away at some carrots. Open on the table was a sky-blue box of chocolates – not Hosuke's, but another one she'd bought just for us. I was sitting with my head propped in my hand, munching away at them while I watched Ginko from behind. I want to try that smock of hers on one day, I thought. I'd have my photo taken, so that I could look back on it in fifty years' time.

"Ginko."

"What?"

"I'm moving out."

"When?"

"Next week. Turns out I can live in the company dormitory."

"That's a bit sudden! *And* you're making it sound like it's got nothing to do with you." She looked around at me, smiling as she wiped her hands on her smock.

"Yeah, sorry."

"Oh, no need to apologise."

"Sure, but . . ."

"It'll be good for you," Ginko said as she carefully arranged the carrots in an earthenware pot. "Striking out on your own like that while you're still young."

I waited for her to go on.

"See, when you're young, that's when—" The doorbell rang. Hosuke was coming over again today. By now he would just stroll in, without us having to let him in. "It's when you learn what real hardship is."

I wanted to ask Ginko when that hardship was coming for me, and what form it would take. And I wanted her to teach me how I was supposed to let it into my life when I had no-one to share it with.

Hosuke abruptly appeared in the kitchen and greeted us with a little bow. Ginko took his coat off for him, gave it a quick brush, then slid it onto a hanger. Soon, I realised, I wouldn't even get to play the third wheel like this.

I wasn't sure I really needed to leave Ginko's house. In fact, I didn't particularly want to. But if I ignored the feeling I had right now, the urge I had to make a go of things on my own, I felt like I'd end up sticking around here forever, and soon enough my life would be over before I'd learned a thing.

The day before I moved out, Ginko made me chirashi sushi. While she mixed the sushi vinegar into the rice, I waved a fan from above to cool it down.

"I thought sushi would be nice. The *zu* in Chizu is the same character as the *su* in sushi, after all!"

"Know why my parents called me Chizu?"

"No, why?"

"Well, the *chi* part means wisdom, right? And *zu* means long life. So, my wisdom is supposed to let me live a long life."

"What a nice name."

"But I still have, like, zero wisdom."

"You think so?"

"Yeah, none. Oh, since moving in here, I did learn that if you stick the lid on a pot upside down you can put another pot on top."

"Well, that's pretty useful."

"Oh, and that people change. Especially the parts you wish would stay the same. And the parts you do wish would change, don't. I wish I knew how to make it the other way round. That's the kind of wisdom I want."

"I don't think that's how it works, Chizu."

Ginko put out a hand to stop me fanning the rice, then started preparing the toppings of chopped-up egg and seasoned fish.

For dessert, she loaded a plate with three pouches of the sweet konnyaku jelly I liked. I remembered that this would be our last dinner together and began to feel a little sad. I chomped away at the jellies one by one, like I was trying to crush that sadness.

After dinner, I'd asked Ginko if she fancied a walk. We set off down the road that led to the supermarket on the other side of the station.

"I hate winter. All this cold. It makes it even harder for me to be nice to people."

"You are nice, Chizu."

"No I'm not. I'm a nasty piece of work."

"Do you want to go to Mount Takao with Hosuke? To eat soba. We decided to postpone our trip to Onahama."

"Oh, you did? Hmm . . . Mount Takao, eh?"

"Only if you feel like it."

"I'm guessing it won't just be me and the old guy. You're coming too, right?"

"Oh, of course."

"Then sure. I mean, I already went in the autumn . . . But yeah, let me know!"

"Alright then. I will!"

I wondered if she really would. Once I moved out, how were we even going to stay in touch? The company dormitory was by Mizuhodai station on the Tojo line, and you had to change trains twice to get there from Ginko's house. There was no way a stay-at-home like Ginko was going to make a trip like that.

We aimlessly perused the aisles of the excessively well-lit supermarket. I dug around in the pocket of my jeans and found the Miffy envelope she had given me for New Year's, all crumpled up. Ginko didn't have her purse with her, so I proudly produced the envelope and said we should buy whatever a thousand yen could get us. We began carefully inspecting the rows of products, one shelf at a time, putting things in our basket only to take them back out again.

Ginko was standing in front of the bananas in the fruit section, seemingly lost in thought.

What *were* her thoughts? How did that brain of hers work? We still knew so little about each other. I still hadn't ever seen her act mean or cruel, and she still had no idea how much nastier I could be when I really wanted. I wondered if maybe we should have made more of an effort with each other. There was probably some deeper relationship we were supposed to have arrived at by now. Without anyone to tell me what was and wasn't possible, I'd probably always feel this uncertain about everything.

Once I got to thinking that way, I began to feel like maybe I should come right out and confess everything. How spiteful I really was, how empty, how troubled. The fact that I'd stolen things from her, things she might well consider precious. Everything. I wanted to know what she thought of it all.

"Strawberries, I reckon," said Ginko in a quiet voice.

"What?"

"Yes. Not bananas. Strawberries."

Ginko walked briskly off towards the strawberries near the entrance. I chased after her and watched her toss the closest pack into the basket.

When we got home, we sat on the veranda and had our strawberries with some soy milk, peanut cream buns and canned yokan.

It was cold, and we'd wrapped blankets around ourselves from the neck down. Trains with almost nobody on them made their usual racket as they sped by. Every time the cold wind picked up, one of us would say, "Let's go in," and yet here we still were. I'd been planning to say something along the lines of, "Thanks for looking after me," but instead a question formed on my lips.

"You know all those pictures of dead cats. The Cherokees. What are you going to do when you get all the way round the room? Like, are you going to start a second layer of them? There's only room for about ten more."

"Oh, I'll be long dead by then."

Right, I thought, convinced by this estimate of her life expectancy. She was old enough that any attempt to insist otherwise would have just sounded flippant.

"What'll happen to the house when you die?"

"You can have it, if you want."

"What? Don't you have any relatives? Brothers and sisters or whatever?"

"I do, but I'm not leaving them the house. They all live too far away."

"Alright then, mine it is. Maybe I'll turn all this into the Secret Garden."

"Just . . . keep the cat photos, okay? No need to put them with me in my coffin or anything."

I imagined Ginko's photo hanging up on the wall after she died, next to all the cats. I wondered whether she, too, would eventually lose her name and become just another dead person, stripped of everything that made her Ginko. Whether a day would come when nobody would even mention her, and all the minor details of her daily life, the food she ate, the clothes she wore, would disappear just like that, as though she'd never existed.

For a while now I'd been feeling Ginko's gaze on my right cheek. I pretended not to notice and carried on chucking the green tops of my strawberries into the garden. "Cold, isn't it," Ginko murmured, and wrapped herself up even more tightly in her blanket.

We'd run out of snacks to eat, and things to say, so I got up and said, "Right, time to run the bath." Maybe it was the cold, but in the brief glimpse I got of Ginko's eyes, they seemed to be glistening slightly.

It was always like this. Goodbyes were much harder when you had time to see them coming.

"Hey, don't cry," I said, then ran off to run the bath.

That evening, sitting among the cardboard boxes in my room, I opened up my shoeboxes.

Recently, the little objects I kept in them had stopped bringing me any comfort. All they did was pull me back inside my memories, providing a crutch for me to dredge up all the pain and the happiness of the past. And yet I couldn't bring myself to throw the boxes away. I had depended on them for too long. I picked one up and gave it a shake, so that the junk inside rattled around drily.

I grabbed the Russian dolls, the green velvet box and the clown doll with the detached head and made my way to Ginko's room. This was the third time I'd sneaked in while she was asleep. By now I was familiar with the noisy sliding door, and knew which floorboards were the creakiest. With bated breath, I returned each of the items I was carrying to their original places. I'd been planning on keeping one of them as a sort of memento, but after pondering my options I began to feel like I didn't want any of them after all.

I sat down at Ginko's side. I hoped the little old lady lying on the futon really would never feel lonely or sad again, but that was probably impossible. Even if she thought she'd used them all up, there was always more where those emotions came from.

"Go back to bed, Chizu."

I gave a little yelp of surprise. "You're awake?"

"Oh yes."

"Since when?"

"Since you came in here."

I just looked at her.

"I was awake that other time too. When you came in and took the doll. Old people don't sleep that deeply, you know."

"So you *were* awake. I had a feeling you might be. Well, I've put everything back."

"Thought you could take the old lady for a ride, eh?"

"Yeah. Sorry about that."

"Silly girl."

"Yeah . . ."

"There was no need to pinch them, you know. I'd have given them to you."

When I explained that I didn't actually want them in the first place, Ginko opened her eyes and chuckled.

"Ginko."

"What?"

"Do you think I'll be okay the way I am?"

Ginko didn't reply. Her gentle gaze passed over my face, shoulders, chest and legs, one after the other, like she was tracing them with a brush. I had the sensation that she was applying a sort of pale tint to each of them in turn.

I repeated my question.

142

"Hmm. That I don't know." Ginko smiled faintly, then turned over so that she was facing away from me.

"But things are tough out there in the real world, aren't they? I feel like I'm just going to fall at the first hurdle."

"There's no *out there* or *in here*, Chizu. There's just the world," Ginko said decisively. I'd never heard her speak that way before. The more I repeated her words in my head, the more I began to feel helpless, like I really didn't know anything.

"Hey. When I leave, will you stick my photo up on the wall?"

"You're not a cat, Chizu."

"Go on, do it."

"But you're not even dead yet."

"You'll forget about me otherwise."

"Oh, those photos aren't where I keep my memories."

Ginko pulled her cover up halfway over her face.

Without checking whether she'd fallen asleep, I went back to my room, sat on my chair and stared at the contents of the shoeboxes again. Then, once I'd had a good look, I pulled my chair up against the wall and climbed onto it. One shoebox at a time, I made my way round each of the Cherokee photos, tucking the objects from the boxes behind their frames. The gym cap, the flower-patterned eraser, the red pen, the strand of hair, the cigarettes, the Jintan mints – everything.

I took the empty shoeboxes, flattened and folded them, bundled them up with a piece of string, then chucked them on top of the pile of old newspapers in the kitchen. Standing by the sink, gazing into the living room from the dark kitchen, my departure from the house felt just as unreal as my arrival.

I pulled one of the bottles of plum wine out from the storage space under the floorboards, drank three glasses of it, then went to bed. Just as I was drifting asleep, the window rattled faintly, and I heard the sound of a train pulling in at the station.

EARLY SPRING

≡◆≡

Whenever I walked out the front door, I always felt like I was forgetting something. No *See you later* when I left, and no *I'm home* when I got back. Come to think of it, I never said those sorts of things when I was living with Ginko either. But now that I was living on my own, I'd become more attuned to their absence.

Every morning, I'd get up, drink the cooled boiled water from the kettle, wash my face, toast some bread, get dressed, do my make-up and go to work. The same routine every day. Sometimes, when I was washing dishes in the kitchen, I'd catch sight of the four little Miffies on my slippers. I always covered my leftovers with a plate rather than cling film, and no matter how many times I tried to make miso soup stock from dried sardines I could never get it quite right.

At night, when sadness slowly crept up on me and I

didn't know what to do with it, I'd start writing Ginko a letter. But I never got any further than "Dear Ginko". The words wouldn't come. Instead, I'd end up doodling things in the corner of the letter paper, maybe a picture of Kuro-jima and Cha-iro, and distract myself that way instead.

A girl my age lived in the room next to mine. On Wednesdays, after work, we'd often go to the cinema together. She worked in a different department, but we became friends after I borrowed a cloth from her to clean the office in the morning. My lunchtimes I spent with Ando, and after work I'd go drinking with other people from my department. Everyone in my office called me by my last name: to them, I was "Mita-chan".

One day, I was waiting for the photocopier when the person in front of me, Mr Sasaki from sales, turned to me.

"Ah, Mita-chan. You've stopped wearing glasses."

"That's right."

"But they suited you."

"Well, it'll be spring soon."

"Oh, I get it. Looking for love, eh?"

"Absolutely."

And so I had replaced the people in my life with new ones. I had thrust myself among people I didn't know. It wasn't a question of being optimistic or pessimistic about life. The days simply rolled into view when I woke up in the morning, and somehow I got through them, one at a time.

By mid-February, there were days when the bitter cold receded slightly. Those were the days when I'd be in a good mood all day long. Before heading into work, I'd take a shower, shave the hair on my upper arms and apply a nice-smelling cream.

And, in a manner of speaking, I'd found someone new.

Soon after I moved into the dormitory, Ando invited me out for drinks with some people from her department, and it was there that I met him. A married man. That was a change. If anything even happened between us, it would mean he was cheating. We exchanged contact details and, with the drinks in us, held hands all the way to the station where we parted ways. He invited me to join him for a meal and a day at the races the following Sunday. It was possible that he really liked me. Still, I told myself that however excited or worried I became, however high my hopes got, things would simply work out the way they worked out.

I didn't yet feel the need to stare endlessly at him or be alone with him like I had with Fujita. Maybe that sort of fiery passion wasn't something I was capable of anymore. But if I worked at it, I reckoned I could probably still get pretty close.

When I looked up from my desk, I'd notice him gazing at me from a distance. How about doing some work, I wanted to tell him. But I wasn't displeased.

No matter how slim the chances were that anything good would come of it, no matter how obvious the ending, there was nothing to stop me starting. It would be spring soon. Surely a bit of recklessness was allowed.

It was Sunday, and the Tojo line train into Tokyo was packed. I was on my way to meet him at the races, just as we'd agreed.

I had my hair down and my face carefully made up. I was still in my winter coat, but my body felt unusually light. I boarded the front carriage of the train, pressed my face to the window next to the driver's compartment, and gazed out at the scenery.

The tracks seemed to carry on in a straight line forever. On each balcony of the housing blocks lining the tracks, people had hung their futons out to dry, as if by some prior arrangement. At one end of a park bloomed the white flowers of a plum tree.

The train was approaching the bridge over the Yanase River. Its banks were lined with slender cherry trees, their branches still bare. In a month or so, they'd be in full bloom, and I'd probably be staring out at them from the packed train into work. A watch on my wrist, pumps on my feet, a black handbag at my side. I watched a boy taking a brown dog for a run, the two of them tracing a line across the grey concrete.

We had agreed to meet at the ticket gates at Fuchu station at eleven. At Ikebukuro I changed to the Saikyo line, and at Shinjuku to the Keio line. I boarded the front carriage of one of the trains that stopped at every station.

148

After a while, the train emerged into daylight, then slowly pulled in at Sasazuka station. The familiar platform slid past the window. Gathered near the kiosk where I'd worked was a gaggle of suntanned girls, racquet bags slung over their shoulders, perhaps on their way to a game. I didn't recognise any of the station attendants on duty, and there was no sight of Fujita, Itoi or Mr Ichijo. When the train doors opened, I got out and looked down the platform. The kiosk was in the central section, a good distance from where I was standing, and I couldn't get a look at whoever was working there now.

When the train moved off again, it began passing through familiar scenery. I stood there in the near-empty carriage, pressing my face right up against the door while a little girl sitting nearby stared curiously at me.

When the driver announced that we were approaching Ginko's station, I pressed my face even harder against the glass door. As the train slowed down, the tall sweet olive tree came into view on the other side of the opposite platform.

There was the house. It hadn't changed at all.

The hedge was as untrimmed as ever, branches poking out here and there. On the laundry pole hung the usual smock and a bath towel. Beyond that, I could only make out half a window, glittering with reflected sunlight. I looked for Ginko's outline in it.

Viewed from the train, the scene seemed frozen in place, like I was looking at a photo backdrop. The smell and feel of life there no longer felt familiar. For a moment, I couldn't even remember how long ago it had been that I'd lived at Ginko's house. I felt like if I went out onto the platform and called to her, it would be years before my voice reached the garden.

The departure bell sounded, and behind me the doors closed again.

Even after the train moved off, I kept my face pressed up against the window, watching the house recede into the distance. Once even the silver glint of the antenna on the roof had disappeared from view, I leaned against the door and, for just a moment, closed my eyes.

The carriage jolted, and the little girl next to me shouted and laughed. I looked down at her and saw that she had taken her shoes off and was standing on the seat, trying to open the window. A woman, presumably her mother, was scolding her while reluctantly helping her with it. When they finally got it open, the wind rushed in. The girl's ponytail bounced around, the hem of her blue skirt fluttering in the breeze.

Without slowing down in the slightest, the train carried me onwards, to a station where someone was waiting.

NANAE AOYAMA, born in 1983, is an acclaimed Japanese fiction writer. Her literary debut, *Light of Windows*, won the Bungei Prize in 2005. Aoyama was awarded the 136th Akutagawa Prize for her novel *A Perfect Day to Be Alone*. Other books include *A Gentle Sigh*, *Fragments*, *Sound of Separation*, *Akari's Lakeside* and *Wind*. Her work has been translated into Chinese, Korean, Vietnamese, German, French and Italian.

JESSE KIRKWOOD is a freelance translator working primarily from Japanese and French into English. In 2020 he was awarded the Harvill Secker Young Translators' Prize for his translation of "Nocturne" by Yūshō Takiguchi. His new translation of Seichō Matsumoto's *Tokyo Express* was published as a Penguin Modern Classic in 2022.